ULTIMA THULE

THE ÆGIS OF MERLIN
BOOK THIRTEEN

JAMES E WISHER

SAND HILL PUBLISHING

CHAPTER 1

Heather James's feet ached as her high heels clicked against the scuffed wooden stage. Flashing lights tried to blind her, and in the process transformed the leering faces of the men in the audience into inhuman masks. She forced a coy smile as the final note of some horrid heavy metal song faded away.

The patrons roared and cheered as she scampered offstage, her G-string stuffed with bills. She paused at the edge, turned back, and blew the crowd a kiss. Whether on the catwalk or a stage, Heather knew how to work a crowd.

As soon as she moved out of sight, her sexy smile twisted into a deep scowl. Goosebumps prickled her porcelain skin in the club's chilly air. You'd think management would keep it warmer in here. Of course, she understood why they didn't. The cold air enhanced certain areas of the female anatomy.

She looked down at her hard nipples and sighed. No one cared about anything beyond her body, her looks. From her days as the world's most popular model down to this, stripping in a Vegas club to the cheers of two-legged pigs, only her beauty ever mattered.

Heaving another sigh, Heather pushed through the door to her dressing room. As the club's headliner, she received certain privileges and a private dressing room was one of them. A few minutes of peace away from the endlessly staring, prying eyes that followed her everywhere helped maintain her sanity. Heather slung a soft silk robe around her shoulders and immediately slumped. Of all the ways she'd envisioned life after her modeling career, long nights spent degrading herself for measly tips from sleazy lowlifes hadn't made the list.

Heather dropped into the chair in front of her mirror and kicked off the painful heels. Makeup brushes and hairspray cans, all cheap generic brands, littered the table. No sign of the Chanel perfumes and Dior lipsticks that used to fill her vanity.

Bracing herself against the table, Heather met her own blue eyes in a mirror surrounded by harsh bulbs. Platinum curls tumbled over her shoulders and full lips gleamed scarlet. Even exhausted, her stunning beauty remained. The face that had once graced magazine covers and floated down haute couture runways was now reduced to gyrating for pocket change in a two-bit strip joint.

The high and mighty Heather James, reduced to this. Talk about pathetic. Hot tears pricked the corners of her eyes. She blinked them back with a snarl that twisted her perfect face into something demonic.

None of this was her fault!

Determination hardened Heather's gaze. She straightened, tossing her hair over her shoulder. The ones responsible for her current misery—Malice Kincade, Conryu Koda, and Maria Kane—would pay for what they did, for reducing her to this. She'd find a way to make them suffer as she had.

Heather laughed at herself. Malice died months ago, depriving her of the chance for revenge, while Conryu had become the most powerful wizard in the world and dedicated himself to Maria's safety. She understood how pathetic she looked lying to herself like this, but the daydreams provided a pleasant distraction all the same.

She changed into jeans and a T-shirt, then collected her money before wrenching the dressing room door open. The dump didn't provide a special entrance for the performers, forcing Heather to stalk across the dance floor and navigate around the perimeter toward the exit. Stale smoke scratched her throat. Raucous chatter and throaty laughter almost drowned out the thumping bass. A trio of half-naked dancers writhed on the platforms. Waitresses wove between tables, balancing trays of overpriced drinks.

At least the current act kept anyone from noticing her. Finally, she reached the exit and stepped out into the dry, desert air. A few deep breaths cleared her lungs.

The bouncer nodded to her as she passed, heading for the parking lot behind the club. Depressing as she found it, Heather looked forward to returning to her modest apartment and washing away the psychic grime.

Heather James…

She spun, lightning crackling around her hands. Anyone mistaking her slim figure for an easy mark would soon regret it. Though she couldn't find work as a wizard—thank you very much, Malice—she stayed in practice and remained more than capable of taking care of herself.

The lot appeared as empty of people as the rest of her life. Heather shook her head. She was losing it.

Her hand hovered inches from the handle of her little black sedan when the same low voice murmured, *I can give you what you want. Power... revenge...*

A shiver ran down her spine. No human voice had ever spoken in that tone. No, "spoken" didn't capture the essence of what she felt. She'd been a wizard long enough to recognize psychic communication.

"Where are you? What are you?"

The voice chuckled, a dark, seductive sound. *I know everything about you, Heather. Your past, your present, and what could be your future. I can give you the means to destroy those who reduced you to this sorry state.*

Heather had never trusted easily, and the last couple of years had done nothing to improve her disposition. "How? And more importantly, what do you want from me in return?"

I can grant you power. More power than you've ever wielded.

Heather snorted. "More power than Conryu Koda, the most powerful wizard in the world? I highly doubt that."

There exist many sorts of power. Mine has a subtler flavor. As for what I want in return, that's simple: I want a pawn I can use to cause chaos on Null's Earth. He does so despise chaos.

Heather didn't trust any of what the demon said. And she had no doubt a demon had somehow contacted her. Still, how much worse could serving a demon be than her current situation?

The demon's psychic laughter echoed in her ears. *Go home and wait. I will reveal everything in time.*

The psychic presence vanished, leaving her truly alone. She pulled the car door open and slid behind the wheel. A few deep breaths calmed her. Lessons from her dark magic classes rushed back. Everything Mrs. Umbra had taught them suggested the path before her would end badly.

But terrible idea or not, she intended to grasp this chance with both hands.

CHAPTER 2

Two days on the floating island allowed Conryu to make a complete recovery from his recent battles with both the Horned One's hellpriest and Abaddon's. The main thing that helped his recovery lay snuggled up beside him in his bed. Maria's head rested on his chest as she slept, her dark hair covering her beautiful face. He brushed the strands aside and wondered, not for the first time, how he'd gotten so lucky.

They'd retreated to his cabin immediately after he finished sorting out the chaos in Central. With no cell service and no way for anyone to reach them, it made for a perfect getaway. Although she had hesitated to be out of contact for the entire weekend, Conryu didn't care. He needed time to recuperate. The world would have to manage on its own for a couple of days. Besides, if the worst happened, even here the Reaper could still contact him through their link.

Maria groaned and looked up at him. "I wish we could stay like this forever."

"You and me both." Conryu kissed her forehead. "Unfortunately, until I've completely eliminated the threat of the demon lords, a couple days at a time is the best we can do."

"Yeah, I know. I guess almost getting killed by a member of our own armed forces has me feeling a bit bitter. Where will you search for the next temple?"

"No idea. In fact, I hoped you might have a suggestion."

Maria sighed and snuggled closer. "Sorry, my research hit a brick wall even before the most recent situation."

"Maybe we'll get lucky and Abaddon's will be the last one."

Her laugh held no hint of humor. "Us and lucky don't go together."

"I don't know. I feel pretty lucky right now." He kissed her again.

An exquisite half hour later, they had dressed and left his cabin. Prime, his demon book familiar, flew out from the back room to join them. Though their minds were connected, he appreciated Prime providing at least the illusion of privacy. For his part, Prime often claimed a distinct lack of interest in closely inspecting human mating customs.

Though Conryu hated to leave their little sanctuary, the time had come to find out what happened out in the world while they recovered.

"Kai."

His ninja bodyguard appeared and bowed. Dressed in all black with only her eyes visible and a sword hilt sticking up by her right ear, Kai was one of the Daughters of the Reaper, his personal force of ninjas. All of them were dark aligned women who had sworn to serve the Reaper and, by extension, Conryu as the Reaper's Chosen.

Conryu summoned the Staff of All Elements and opened

the door to his enchanted library. As soon as they entered, Conryu willed them to shift to the hall outside the Kanes' apartment. An instant later, he and Maria stepped out.

"Back in the real world," she sighed. "I'll change and head to the Department. Maybe I can come up with a target for you."

"That would be fantastic." He kissed her one last time. "Love you."

"Love you too. Stay safe."

If only that option existed in his line of work. She unlocked the door and slipped inside. Only then did Kai join him in the hall. He sealed the library, and the door vanished.

"What now, Chosen?"

"I need to make a quick trip to Heaven." Prime groaned, but Conryu was accustomed to his distaste and ignored him. "Then we'll swing by the monastery to see how Kanna and the girls are doing. I have a surprise planned that I think they'll enjoy."

She cocked her head but only asked, "Do you wish me to join you?"

"No, it won't take long, and I can go straight from Heaven to the monastery. I'll meet you there."

She bowed and vanished into the borderland. She usually insisted on accompanying him everywhere. Maybe she'd started to lighten up a little.

"Maybe she wants to avoid visiting the awful place," Prime said.

"Kai's human, just dark aligned. She shouldn't suffer any ill effects from visiting Heaven."

"Lucky her," Prime said.

Conryu rolled his eyes and opened a heaven portal.

———

Conryu's brief stop in Heaven lasted only a few minutes. The Goddess had not seemed thrilled with his request, but ultimately she granted him permission and explained how to perform the magic he had in mind. He felt confident the girls would enjoy his surprise.

He stepped out of another portal and into the courtyard of the old monastery which served as headquarters for the Daughters of the Reaper. Made of dark-gray stone and consisting of a number of interconnected buildings which served as barracks and storage for their weapons and supplies, the monastery had ended up being a perfect fit, especially the location. Calling it off the beaten path would be an understatement. Situated in the mountains of the Land of the Night Princes, you'd struggle to find somewhere more remote.

No sooner had Conryu's feet touched the courtyard dirt than scores of black-clad figures appeared, kneeling in perfect unison. Despite having been together for over three years now, having his own force of totally obedient ninjas still struck him as strange. Nevertheless, he'd become quite fond of them and did his best to keep them safe. Pity his work didn't always allow it.

Kai appeared beside him and asked, "How did your meeting go?"

"Good. The Goddess approved, albeit reluctantly, the treat I planned for everyone."

"A treat?" Kai asked.

"You'll see."

Grandmaster Kanna emerged from one of the side buildings and strode over. She bowed and said, "Chosen, how may we serve?"

"I've got some special training planned. Is this everyone not out on a mission? It seems like we're a bit short of people."

"The master had a task for us, so three squads are off taking care of it."

Conryu frowned. "I didn't realize the Reaper gave you direct orders."

"He doesn't often, but now and then something comes up. Did you not notice that our numbers often change? That's because new members join while others go on missions for the master. Sometimes a Daughter is called to Black City during those missions."

He hadn't thought much about it but couldn't say it came as a surprise. "What are they doing now?"

"Hunting down stray hellfire warlocks in Central America. It's good training for them, and the master wants no survivors of the sect lingering on his Earth. Do you need me to call them back?"

"No, it's fine. I was just surprised. This training might become a regular thing, so they'll have another chance."

He turned to face the gathered ninjas. "Today, your skills will be put to the test. I've arranged for a special guest instructor, an elven warrior who will spar with you one-on-one and then offer critiques of your techniques and suggest areas for improvement."

One of the girls, Tamaki unless he missed his guess, stared right at him. He winked at her. Kai had mentioned she wanted to duel one of his elf warriors but felt too shy to ask. Hopefully she'd have fun today. After all her hard work over the last few months, she deserved it.

He raised the staff and a glowing white heaven portal opened. Under his breath, he murmured, "Sho."

It felt weird calling his father by his first name, but the only way to summon a specific elf rather than the whole squad was to name them.

A tall figure strode out of the portal, clad in silver armor, a slightly curved sword hanging at his side. Conryu's father, once human but now transformed into an elven warrior, entered the courtyard with supernatural grace. His pointed ears made his race clear, even if the armor failed to.

Dad paused beside him. "I never expected to teach again."

"The girls already fight well, but I figured you could give them a few pointers." Turning to the gathered Daughters, he said, "Tamaki, do you want to go first? Also, we'll need some practice swords."

Tamaki stood and joined them while another girl jogged off to fetch wooden swords. "I am honored that you granted my wish, Chosen. Also, Kai talks too much."

Conryu grinned. That might be the first time he'd ever heard anyone accuse one of the Daughters of talking too much.

"You should've told me yourself. I like doing nice things for you guys once in a while. I'm not worried you'll get soft."

The second girl returned with the wooden swords and handed one to Tamaki and one to his father.

"Let's keep the round to three minutes. That way, everyone will have a chance to practice." Conryu, Kai, and Kanna moved to a safe distance. Then he said, "Ready? Begin!"

Tamaki and Dad came together with a clack of wood. Tamaki went on the offense, vanishing and reappearing in rapid succession in an attempt to throw Dad off.

She might as well have not bothered. He blocked every strike while barely shifting one way or the other. It looked so effortless, as if he didn't have to try.

Conryu kind of pitied Tamaki. Given his father's skill, the fight seemed almost unfair.

Two minutes in, as if he'd seen everything he needed to, Dad went on the offense. A quick thrust and slash drove Tamaki back on her heels.

A final flick of his wrist sent her wooden sword flying to clatter on the stones.

"Okay," Conryu said. "That's good for this match."

He rejoined the pair. Tamaki panted for breath, but his father remained utterly at ease.

"I never…" Tamaki said between gasps. "How did you block my strikes so easily?"

"I can sense when you're about to reappear. That makes it easy to know where you plan to attack. That skill of yours is impressive, but to someone aware of what's coming, all you're doing is warning your enemy. Something to keep in mind going forward."

"I will." Tamaki bowed. "Thank you for the instruction."

Before calling the next Daughter, Conryu leaned in. "Did the match live up to your expectations?"

"Yes, Chosen, thank you. If ever my ego grows too large, I will remember this day."

He prepared to call the next girl when his phone rang. Muttering unkind things, he fished it out of his pocket. The president's number flashed on the screen. "Sir?"

"Conryu, we have a situation."

Well, he'd been off the floating island for an hour. Naturally a new problem had cropped up. "What's going on?"

"A report just came in of a kraken fighting a flying ship over the Pacific."

Conryu stared at his phone. Surely he'd misheard. "What?"

"I know it sounds crazy," the president said. "But there's a cargo ship caught in the fight, and they're in trouble. The Empire of the Rising Sun contacted me and requested I forward their request for aid to you. Can you help?"

"The kraken suggests Dagon's involvement, Master," Prime said. "As for the flying ship, I have no idea."

"I'm on my way. Thanks for the heads-up." Conryu ended the call and turned to face the Daughters. They all watched him with expectant eyes.

"Sorry everyone, training's canceled. An emergency's come up. Kanna, I need two squads. Tamaki, you're with me and Kai."

While Kanna made her selection, he walked his father over to the still-open heaven portal. "I'm going to have to cut your visit short, Dad. Duty calls."

"As it always does. If you need us, son, don't hesitate." His father stepped through the portal and returned to Heaven.

Two groups of four ninjas separated themselves from the gathering while Tamaki returned her black iron sword to her back. It looked like they were ready.

To possibly fight a kraken and some sort of flying ship.

Just thinking it sounded nuts. But then again, he'd seen some weird stuff over the last year. Probably best not to overthink things. He'd deal with whatever he had to no matter how weird the threat. He opened a hell portal and entered the borderland.

CHAPTER 3

Once Conryu and his team appeared in the borderland, where time virtually stopped, he took a moment to brief everyone on what lay ahead. None of the ninjas so much as batted an eye at the idea of fighting an unknown flying ship and a kraken. He sometimes wondered what it would take to shake the Daughters, but he had yet to come up with anything.

"Securing the cargo vessel takes priority. Kai, Tamaki, and I will handle that. If the ship and kraken flee, I want the backup squads to follow them." He looked each girl in the eye. "Under no circumstances should you engage the targets. Understand?"

After they all bowed in acknowledgment, he focused on the first group. "Team one, you'll follow the kraken. I assume it'll dive when it flees. Will following it underwater from the borderland pose a problem?"

"No, Chosen," said the ninja he assumed served as the team leader. "We won't be able to shift to the mortal realm to attack, but observation only will be no problem."

"Perfect." He turned his attention to the second group. "Team two, I'm confident you won't have any trouble following the flying ship no matter how fast it moves, but be careful all the same."

They bowed a second time.

The vastness of the Pacific Ocean combined with the president's rather vague directions made finding the cargo ship a problem. Luckily for Conryu, he had the best tracker in the world on his side.

"Cerberus?" The huge three-headed demon dog barked when Conryu called his name. "I need you to find a giant squid for me. Can you do that?"

Cerberus sniffed the air and oriented himself before barking again.

"Good boy." Conryu flew up on his back, and Kai and Tamaki joined him a moment later. "Let's hunt!"

Cerberus took off like a rocket, racing through the endless darkness of the borderland. Given the total lack of landmarks, Conryu had a poor sense of distance, but all too soon, Cerberus stopped and barked again.

Conryu flew down and opened a viewing portal. Back on Earth, wind and rain lashed a floundering cargo ship. Lightning crackled and thunder rumbled. From below the waves, eight tentacles rose over a hundred feet into the air.

A single-masted ship lacking a sail flew just out of reach of the grasping tentacles. It reminded Conryu of a cat trying to reach a toy dangling just out of reach. On the deck at the front of the ship, a figure dressed in Roman-style armor hurled a lightning bolt at a massive tentacle. The spell singed the slimy appendage but caused no other damage. Looked like a stalemate for now.

He shifted the portal for a better look at the cargo ship. It listed badly. Nothing short of a miracle would keep it upright for more than fifteen minutes.

"Kai, Tamaki, we need to get the sailors off that ship. I have no idea how those two will react when we arrive, so stay alert. The rest of you know what to do."

He shifted again, positioning them right next to the canted walkway leading to the ship's bridge, and opened a portal.

As soon as he stepped onto the walkway, he conjured a barrier to keep the rain off him and Prime. The wind did its best to deafen him as it tried to fling him into the ocean. Conryu narrowed his eyes and could just make out corrupt flakes drifting through the storm. That confirmed his suspicion that magic had created the storm. Though whether the kraken or the spellcaster caused it, he couldn't tell.

Three strides brought him to the bridge door. A gesture blasted it off its hinges. Inside, the sailors all looked his way. An all-Asian crew. Not a surprise, since the Empire of the Rising Sun wasn't known for its multiculturalism.

"Call your crew up here," Conryu said. "I'll get you to safety."

They continued to stare at him.

He tried again in Japanese, and this time the man at the helm asked, "Who are you?"

"Conryu Koda. Your government requested my help. Now—"

The kraken loosed a guttural bellow that shook Conryu to his bones. It dove beneath the frothing waves, and a moment later, the flying ship made a hasty retreat northeast. The girls would follow them. Right now, he needed to focus on getting these people to safety.

A huge wave, created when the kraken dove, crashed over

the deck as the crew scrambled around. The freighter didn't have a chance and they had to know it.

"Unless you want to go down with the ship, I suggest you hurry." Lowering his voice, he added, "Kai, Tamaki, check for stragglers. I don't want to leave anyone behind."

The man he took to be the captain shouted orders into a microphone. The crew on deck scrambled toward them, climbing up to the bridge as fast as they could.

Conryu opened a heaven portal and waved them through. The sailors hesitated, but a particularly powerful lurch convinced them to take their chances with the unknown portal.

When only Conryu and the captain remained on the bridge, the deck had tilted so much that he had to activate a flying spell to hold his position.

"Is that everyone?"

"Yes." The captain struggled to reach the portal.

Conryu grabbed him with an ethereal hand and tossed him through.

"Kai?"

Her disembodied voice said, "We searched the ship. There are no others aboard."

He sighed in relief. "Great. I'll meet you in the empire."

With that, he flew through the portal and emerged amidst the drifting clouds of Heaven. They appeared well away from the golden gates where he usually arrived. No sense troubling the locals with unexpected guests.

The sailors gaped, disbelief stamped all over their faces. Visiting Heaven for the first time could definitely have that effect on a person.

Conryu flew over to the captain. "Which port would you like me to take you to?"

"Matsushima. Is this…?"

"Heaven, yeah. The very outer edge. It's the safest of the spirit realms for mortals to visit. Does anyone need healing? There's no better place for it."

"We're okay, sir."

Conryu smiled. "Great. If you could gather your men and link arms to form a human chain, I'll transport us to your destination. Just picture the docks in as much detail as you can. Since I've never visited the place, your memories will guide us."

It didn't take long for the well-trained crew to gather and link arms. Conryu took his place at the front of the line and placed a hand on the captain's shoulder. He connected their minds on a surface level and then willed them to the place in the captain's head. Once a viewing window confirmed they'd reached the right location, he opened a portal and guided the men through.

Conryu came out last and found the crew staring in wonder. Some had dropped to their knees to kiss the rough boards beneath their feet.

At the captain's barked order, the crew scrambled to their feet, formed a neat line, and bowed to him. When they straightened, Conryu approached the captain and held out his hand.

They shook, and Conryu asked, "Will you be okay from here?"

"Yes, the company offices are just down the docks. Thank you again for saving my crew, Koda-san."

"My pleasure, Captain. Best of luck to you all." Conryu renewed his flying spell and shot into the air. Now that he'd delivered everyone safely, he needed to make a call.

He hit the president's number and got an answer after only one ring. "Conryu, what's the situation?"

"Under control." Conryu gave him a quick report. "The cargo ship's crew came through okay, but the ship's a total loss."

"And the others?"

"Not sure yet. They split not long after I arrived. Looking into them is my next task. I'll keep you updated as I can."

"Much appreciated, Conryu."

He disconnected and pocketed his phone. He doubted anyone would have any news yet, but he could wait to hear from them in the borderland.

CHAPTER 4

Conryu yawned as he floated in the endless darkness of the borderland. Despite enjoying two good days of rest, he still felt a bit tired. It wouldn't bother him in a fight, but with nothing here to amuse him, the battle to keep his eyes open raged. He stayed near the edge of the mortal realm, allowing time to run close to normal.

He didn't know how much time had passed when a distant glow caught his eye. The flicker of movement soon resolved into the shapes of four ninjas. Directions meant little here, so he couldn't tell which team approached. As much as he disliked waiting, it seemed too soon for them to return.

The girls stopped a little ways away and bowed.

"What happened?" Conryu asked.

"The ship vanished, Chosen," the team leader said.

Conryu cocked his head. "Could you elaborate?"

"I don't know how else to describe it. We kept pace without issue, and then it disappeared as if it had never existed. We searched the immediate area but sensed nothing amiss."

"That's weird. Take me to where you last saw it."

She nodded and guided them through the borderland. Soon enough they stopped and the leader said, "Here, Chosen."

He opened a viewing portal and looked around at the icy, desolate tundra. Nothing of note stood out in any direction. He really didn't want to venture into that frigid wasteland. Even with magic protecting him it was going to suck. But he saw no way around it and sitting around thinking about it wouldn't accomplish anything.

"I'll keep watch for frost giants, Master," Prime said.

Conryu hadn't considered the possibility of one showing up, but he nodded. "Thanks."

Wrapping himself in a bubble of heated air, Conryu left the borderland. The wind pushed against him, and he shivered despite feeling perfectly comfortable in his bubble.

Okay, where did you go?

He scanned the barren landscape, reaching out with his magical senses, but found nothing. No sign of the mysterious flying ship or of a pocket dimension.

"What do you think, pal? I'm getting nothing."

"I sense nothing either," Prime said. "Whatever magic they used left no lingering presence. If I had to guess, I'd say a large-scale invisibility spell."

"Huh. Well, I guess we'll have to approach it from another angle." He returned to the borderland and addressed the team leader. "You guys can join up with the kraken squad for now. I need to figure out what the hell is going on. Oh, before you go, I didn't catch your name."

"Linna, Chosen. I had the honor of serving you during the fight with Abaddon's hellpriest."

"Right, I remember. Sorry for not recognizing you. Your uniforms all kind of blend together. Off you go."

With a final bow, Linna's team vanished into the borderland.

"Time to pay Maria a visit," Conryu said. "Maybe she can find something."

The trip to Central City took only moments, and soon Conryu stepped into the familiar dimness of the parking garage which generally served as his arrival point. The tang of gasoline and oil hung especially thick in the air today. It smelled like someone needed a tune-up. Across the street stood the imposing black office building that housed the Department of Magic. He couldn't remember how many times he'd visited the place, but nothing good ever seemed to happen when he did.

He left the parking garage, crossed the street, and pushed through the glass doors. The lobby secretaries glanced up as he passed, but they all knew him, and more importantly, they understood it was best not to ask why he dropped by. Conryu waved as he headed for the elevators, relieved not to have to explain today's visit since the ladies would likely think he'd lost his mind.

He jabbed the button for Maria's floor. As soon as the doors slid open and he entered the hall, a dark shape materialized before him.

"Chosen. All has been quiet here," Jen said.

Conryu let out a breath. He still had Jen and her team keeping an eye on Mr. Kane. He doubted Maria's father would intentionally cause him trouble, but he'd lost a lot of faith in the government lately, so better safe than sorry.

"Thanks, Jen. Keep up the good work."

She bowed and melted back into the borderland without a sound. Conryu strode down the hallway to Maria's office. The tapping of a keyboard emerged from behind her partly open door. She was here, perfect.

He knocked then slipped inside. Maria looked up as he approached, a little frown turning her lips down.

"Conryu? Is everything okay? I didn't expect to see you again so soon."

He grabbed a spare chair, dragged it over, and sat down. "I didn't expect to be here again so soon, but some things happened. Are you free to do a bit of research?"

"Of course. The Department pays me, but everyone knows I basically work for you. What happened?"

He laid it all out, and when he finished, Maria gaped at him. "If anyone else told me that story, I'd call for a padded ambulance."

"A not-at-all-unreasonable response, but rest assured it's all true. The girls are tracking the kraken, but I have no idea where the flying ship went."

"Are you sure it's Roman?" she asked.

"I'm sure the guy flinging lightning bolts from the front of it was dressed just like a general from that movie we watched last year. Granted, the historical accuracy of a Hollywood blockbuster might not meet the highest standard, but I figure it had to be close."

"Well, let's ask the internet." She typed in a search for Roman sailing ships.

After a moment, images of ancient ships filled the screen, their wooden hulls and billowing sails contrasting sharply with the sleek metal of modern vessels.

"See anything that matches?"

"Not on this page. Keep going."

Maria clicked through eight pages of images before he pointed and said, "That one. It's the closest match to what I saw."

Maria clicked on the image, enlarging it. The ship's prow curled into a decorative design, oars jutted from its sides, and a single white sail hung from the mast.

"It didn't have oars or a sail, but everything else looks the same."

"Hmm, the website hosting the image is Historical Conspiracies. Not sure how much faith we should put in a conspiracy site. It says here it's a Roman exploratory vessel, allegedly one of those sent to map the edges of the known world, particularly a region called Ultima Thule."

"Never heard of it," Conryu said.

"Me neither."

"Can you do some more digging? Maybe find something more reliable than… this." He waved at the site just as a popup appeared offering Ancient Greek supplements at seventy percent off.

"Sure, no problem. I wasn't having much luck with my other inquiries anyway."

"Thanks, Maria." He stood and kissed the top of her head.

"Where are you going?" she asked.

He grinned. "I'm going fishing."

———

Gaius Varro relaxed a fraction once the ship transformed into its ethereal form. Invisible, silent, and untraceable, he could now safely head back to base. His new master would not be pleased with this failure, but he had followed his orders, so Lord Calint couldn't get too angry—or so he liked to think. His former master, the late Emperor Severus, often raged when things didn't go as he desired, regardless of how well one followed orders.

Gaius preferred his current master's logical nature. The man—assuming the word "man" applied to a dark elf sorcerer—made plans, followed through, and seldom acted on a whim. It made for a pleasant change of pace.

Gaius slammed a fist on the helm. The twenty shark-men seated where a team of oarsmen would normally sit looked his way, their dark, slightly glowing eyes reminding him of their demonic nature. His inability to harm Dagon's monster both frustrated and annoyed him. His most powerful lightning bolt barely singed the beast. The plan required him to kill the guardian then deploy his troops to collect Narukami Tempest's temple core from its place on the ocean floor. Disgust warred with rage when he thought of his weakness. Best not to think too hard about the master's reaction when he found out what happened.

He shook his head; thinking about it would only make him angrier. Since his transformation into a hellstorm warlock, his temper had worsened significantly. In fact, it had taken him most of a century to bring it under control.

Gaius looked down at the dense jungle. Not much farther to the fortress. From there, he could transport them to Narukami Tempest's temple. He guided the ship lower until he spotted a particular patch of dense growth. If you didn't know what to look for, you might never notice any difference from the rest of the jungle canopy. His ethereal ship passed through without issue and came to a stop a few feet above the courtyard of a walled fortress.

Once the ship solidified, he said, "Everyone out."

The shark-men tossed rope ladders over the side and climbed down. Gaius simply leaped out and used wind magic to slow his descent. When his troops finished disembarking, he led them into the central tower, an all-steel monstrosity that rose nearly as high as the surrounding trees.

He paid little attention to the empty halls as he climbed to the top floor. There he found a single room with a complex spell circle drawn on the floor.

"Gather around!" Gaius said.

When the shark-men had crowded into the circle, Gaius used his key to activate it, which instantly transported them all to a field near the temple.

Narukami Tempest's unique flavor of corruption washed over him. He felt welcome here in a way he never had anywhere else. He turned toward the dark stone temple perched on a nearby cliff overlooking the ocean. A very special storm raged over the temple, its magic serving to hide it from anyone who didn't know how to find it.

Gaius marched toward the waiting temple. The doors opened as he approached, and two of his fellow hellstorm warlocks waited just inside. They snapped to attention as he passed and said, "Strength and honor."

He nodded back. "Strength and honor."

Once they entered, the shark-men broke off and headed for their barracks, where they would wait for their next chance to retrieve the temple core. Unless Lord Calint had devised a new plan to defeat the kraken, Gaius had no idea how they would proceed.

He reached the chapel and grimaced at the sight of the massive guardian demon looming over the altar. Over eight feet tall and covered in plates of dark armor shot through with crackling lightning, the demon looked like a nightmare brought to life. Though they all served the same master, the demon's presence always put him on edge.

Lord Calint meditated on the floor in front of the altar. Dressed in a dark robe, with his legs folded under him, the dark elf appeared far too small and frail to pose a threat, but Gaius had learned the hard way when they first met that appearances often deceived.

The dark elf opened one black eye and looked at him. "You failed."

"Yes, my lord. The kraken resisted my strongest magic without taking any noticeable damage. When the Reaper's Chosen appeared, we fled as ordered rather than risk conflict."

"Disappointing but unsurprising. I am in the process of locating a power source of sufficient strength to kill the kraken. Once I home in on its position, you will retrieve it."

Gaius bowed. "I await your command, my lord."

Lord Calint closed his eye, and Gaius took that as his cue to leave. Whatever weapon he sought must possess tremendous power to kill something as massive as the kraken. Gaius could hardly wait to get his hands on it.

———

Racing through the darkness on Cerberus, Conryu and his companions soon caught up with the teams assigned to kraken detail. The girls flew along at a brisk pace, confirming that the target hadn't yet reached its destination. Assuming it had a destination. For all Conryu knew, the damn thing just swam around all the time. He doubted that, but until it stopped, he could only guess.

As Cerberus trotted alongside the teams, he asked, "What news?"

"None, Chosen," the leader of the first team said. He made a mental note to ask her name later. "The beast swims endlessly and seemingly at random near the ocean floor. We've checked, and even in places miles deep, it never leaves the bottom."

"Weird." Conryu opened a viewing portal and enhanced his vision. Sure enough, the kraken swam lazily along, its tentacles trailing behind it, seeming without a care in the world. The creature had to measure five hundred feet long. Barnacles covered its thick, rubbery skin and it undulated in a way that left him queasy.

Conryu frowned as he studied the monstrous creature. What game was it, or more likely its master, playing? He had no clue, and that annoyed him immensely.

He couldn't dive down and interrogate a giant squid, and fighting it in its element would pose a problem. Best to wait and watch—for now.

"Hey, Prime, can that thing sense our presence? If it knows someone's on its tail, it might hesitate to return home."

"Highly unlikely, Master," Prime said. "If we were watching from Dagon's hell, it might sense something, but from here, it's almost impossible."

"Almost?" Conryu asked.

"Since even I don't know with absolute certainty what a demon beast dedicated to Dagon can do, I didn't want to mislead you."

Conryu appreciated Prime's rare show of modesty.

"Why not just destroy the beast now and be done with it?" Tamaki asked.

"Two reasons. First, fighting that thing underwater would put me at a huge disadvantage. I could probably kill it, but you guys wouldn't be able to help. If you appeared at these depths, you'd end up crushed in an instant. Second, if that kraken belongs to Dagon, I want it to lead us to his temple. Assuming an underwater temple exists."

Tamaki didn't seem especially pleased with his answer. Hell, Conryu wasn't thrilled with it either, but for now, they would have to be patient.

"Look, as long as that thing doesn't go on a rampage, we've got time. It's bound to lead us somewhere interesting eventually." He didn't add "hopefully," but he suspected they could hear it in his tone.

"As you say, Chosen," Tamaki said.

"Good." He turned back to the observation teams. "Keep watching and let me know as soon as it stops, or heaven forbid, if it comes to the surface."

He received a chorus of "Yes, Chosen," then left the girls to their pursuit. He wondered who would contact him first, the girls or Maria.

CHAPTER 5

The door creaked shut behind Heather, plunging her modest apartment into darkness. Unable to make out any details, she imagined she had returned to her old penthouse apartment—the amazing view, beautiful art on the walls, and luxury furniture. It had been a home worthy of a princess.

And now she lived here. A quick flick of the switch revealed the living room in all its modest glory. She flung her bag onto the threadbare armchair and looked around. What was the demon waiting for? She paced barefoot across the living room floor.

The evil thing had said to go home and wait. How long did the demon expect her to wait? As soon as the thought formed, she realized it didn't matter. She didn't have any pressing business on her agenda.

Memories of the demon's voice echoed in her mind. Could she trust it? Of course not. Only fools trusted a demon. No, forget trust. Would it grant her the power it promised? As long as she worded the contract properly and the demon agreed, then yes, it should. But with demons things seldom went as expected. She vastly preferred dealing with water spirits.

Hours dragged by and doubt crept in, insidious doubts that whispered she'd lost her grip on reality. The stress and depression had finally pushed her over the edge and she'd started hearing things, imagining things that would tell her what she wanted to hear.

Maybe she was going crazy. At this point, losing her mind would be a relief.

Exhausted and bitter, Heather dragged herself to the bedroom, ready to collapse onto her lumpy mattress. The moment she touched the handle, a chill ran down her spine that had nothing to do with the room's temperature.

She froze.

Your lack of patience will be a problem. The demon's voice sounded displeased.

"Was that little delay a test then?" Heather snapped, bristling. Everyone always jerked her around, even demons.

Everything is a test, mortal. And while you may have failed this one, you're still my best option. For now.

"Who the hell are you? What are you?" Heather asked. "Enough screwing around. You want me to serve you or whatever, level with me."

As you wish. I am Ardent Lilly, Lady of Lust. The voice purred, almost seductive.

Heather's brow furrowed. The name meant nothing to her. Sounded like a succubus. No, that didn't make sense. No succubus would dare cause trouble for the Reaper.

You compare me to a succubus? And one of Null's at that? How insulting. I'll have you know I'm a demon lord. I rule an entirely different hell.

Nothing the voice said made any sense to Heather. But whatever. If Ardent Lilly could give her the power she needed to claim her revenge, nothing else mattered.

"What do you want from me?"

Your hatred for the Reaper's Chosen drew my attention. I've watched you, studied you for months. I'm quite confident that you, Heather James, are the perfect choice to serve as my agent on Earth.

Agent? More like a slave. The idea of serving anyone made Heather's skin crawl. After all the betrayals, becoming anyone's servant didn't appeal to her.

"And if I don't want to be your agent?" she asked.

Ardent Lilly laughed, as chilling a sound as Heather had ever heard. *Then by all means, continue on with your pathetic existence. Stripping for pocket change, wallowing in misery and self-pity. It's all most of you mortals are good for in any case.*

The demon's words stung, each one a tiny barb stabbing at Heather's meager remaining pride. Her life was in shambles; she couldn't deny it. "What exactly does being your agent entail?"

It entails whatever I decide it entails. You will become my instrument, performing the tasks I set for you. The first one requires you to set a trap for the Reaper's Chosen. And when he walks into it, you will crush him.

Heather offered a humorless laugh. She'd followed Conryu's exploits, what little she could find online. The idea of her crushing him was absurd, no matter the power boost.

Though I lack a temple on Earth, I can still grant you the power you'll need. And remember, this is a trap we're setting, not a straight-up fight. Much as it pains me, I admit that even with my help, you'd have no hope of defeating him in such a situation. But with the right circumstances, victory is possible.

"I assume all these wonderful gifts come with a cost."

To complete the contract, you'll need to trade your soul.

Heather's breath caught in her throat. Trade her soul? She'd learned about soul contracts at the Academy, but no sane wizard used them anymore. Other, safer ways existed to make deals with demons. As if reading her thoughts, Ardent Lilly spoke again.

My connection to Earth is tenuous at best. A soul contract is the only thing powerful enough to bridge the gap between our realms. Even maintaining this conversation taxes my strength and, worst of all, risks drawing Null's attention.

Heather clenched her fists until her nails bit into her palms. She couldn't bear the idea of losing this chance and continuing her miserable existence. Consequences be damned. She wouldn't allow this opportunity to slip away.

"What do I need to do?" she asked.

Finally found your spine? Good, you'll need it. The process is simple. Write a contract pledging your soul to me. Sign it with a bloody fingerprint, then burn it to ash to complete the ritual.

Heather nodded. She could do that. "When should I perform the ritual?"

As soon as possible. And once you do, it will be necessary for you to keep up appearances until the time is right. Don't worry, it won't be very long. I'll be in touch.

The weight of Ardent Lilly's regard vanished. Did the demon trust her to complete the contract on her own? That struck her as strange until she remembered her soul had to be given of her own free will. Perhaps pressuring her would be enough to make the spell fail.

Heather blew out a sigh. Eager—well, maybe not eager,

but determined—as she felt, she planned to take a little time to ensure she had no doubts. This wasn't the sort of thing you could take back later.

CHAPTER 6

Maria squinted at the glowing screen, the bright light jabbing her tired eyes. The more time she spent reading articles on History's Conspiracies, the closer she came to developing a headache. A few of the articles were well done, albeit a little off the wall, but others—heaven's mercy, a well-trained chimpanzee could write more coherent prose.

She scrolled through another wall of frenzied text, completely lacking punctuation, until the words became a blur. She rubbed her tired eyes. This was getting ridiculous. Leaving the cursed site, she searched for the Central City University page. Surely she could find something more reliable there.

From the home page, she clicked on the history department and hello! Dr. Julian Palmer, Professor of Ancient Roman History. He sounded like the person she needed to speak to.

She snatched her phone and dialed the department's number, her knee bouncing as it rang.

"History Department," a woman's voice said. "How may I help you?"

Maria introduced herself and asked, "May I speak with Dr. Palmer, please?"

After a brief pause, the woman replied, "He should be between classes at the moment. Let me transfer you."

Maria gave a silent fist pump. So far, so good.

Eventually, a male voice said, "Dr. Palmer speaking."

"Hi, Professor. I'm Maria Kane, a researcher with the Department of Magic. I'm looking into some unusual historical leads and hoped to consult with you. Do you have any availability today?"

"Hmm, let me check. I have an opening at four this afternoon after my last class if that works for you, Ms. Kane."

"Four is perfect, thank you. I'll see you then." Maria hung up, a grin spreading across her face. With any luck, a real expert could shed some light on the mysterious Ultima Thule.

Not wanting to sound completely ignorant going into the meeting, Maria dove into the web. She speed-read through all of the legitimate articles she could find on Ultima Thule. Most of it read like a myth, a bit of fiction rather than history. Well, the legend of the kraken turned out to be plenty real. Maybe this would too.

She found fragmentary tales of a legendary northern realm, forever out of reach. The Romans had launched expeditions into the mists, chasing whispers and shadows in search of a land that couldn't be found. Most interestingly, after the fall of Rome, no other society picked up the quest, likely because the Dark Ages began and no one had the resources to chase legends.

Maria jotted down questions for Dr. Palmer across her

notepad. The trick involved asking them in a way that didn't make her sound as crazy as the conspiracy theorists. The more she read, the more confident she became that something magical was involved in the mystery of Ultima Thule. Exactly what sort of magic, on the other hand, she had no idea.

Maria checked the clock. Wow, half an hour until her meeting. Time to get going. She grabbed her bag and headed to the parking lot. She'd go straight home after speaking with the professor.

The drive to the university didn't take long since less than a mile separated it from the Department. She parked behind a gray stone building with a sign that read History Hall.

Students streamed out the front door, chatting happily about whatever they'd been studying or, more likely, gossiping about campus life. For a moment, Maria missed the Academy. Not that she'd done much gossiping, she'd been too focused on her studies, but that had been a somewhat more peaceful time—at least between disasters.

When the stream of students ended, she slipped through the door. Inside, she found a handy map of the building. Dr. Palmer's room was labeled. She memorized the number and set out through the unfamiliar halls. The scent of old books hung in the air, making her feel at home.

Soon enough she reached room 204. Dr. Palmer's name gleamed on the frosted glass, and Maria paused to collect herself. After a deep breath, she knocked twice.

"Come in!" a man's voice said.

She pushed the door open and controlled chaos greeted her. Bookshelves strained under the weight of leather-bound tomes, while a replica Roman bust surveyed the clutter with an imperious gaze. Rising from behind a desk overflowing with papers was, she assumed, Dr. Julian Palmer. He looked younger than she expected, maybe in his late thirties, with a strong jawline and deep-set brown eyes framed by wire-rimmed glasses. His dark hair, neatly combed and trimmed short, gave him an almost military vibe. He wore a crisp button-down shirt tucked into tailored slacks that both argued he came from money.

He had a far more orderly personal appearance than he did an office.

"Ms. Kane, I presume?" He offered a firm handshake and a wry smile. "I believe this is the first time someone from the Department of Magic has shown an interest in Ancient Roman history."

Maria smiled and settled into the chair across from him. "Our interests depend on current threats in the magical world and thus change constantly. Before we begin, I wanted to thank you for fitting me in on such short notice."

"Not at all. I'm always happy to be of service. So, what can I help you with?"

Maria leaned forward. "I'm interested in Ultima Thule. Was it more than a myth?"

"Ultima Thule doesn't refer to a specific place; it roughly translates to a place beyond the world's known boundaries. To ancient cartographers, that simply meant beyond the land they'd already mapped. A more layman's take generally refers to an area north of the Kingdom of the Isles. The Romans believed they'd find another island there, but they never did."

"I've located records indicating expeditions launched but never returned."

"And you think something magical happened to them?"

"I can't go into detail for obvious security reasons, but yes, that's our working theory."

"How interesting. The Romans were relentless in their pursuits, Ms. Kane. They conquered the known world and continually pushed the boundaries of their maps. But Ultima Thule eluded them until the empire fell. Most serious scholars consider it fantasy."

"And what do you think, Professor?"

"I don't know, but I like to keep an open mind." He stood, walked over to a bookshelf, and pulled down a worn volume. When he found the page he wanted, he continued. "The last recorded expedition launched under Emperor Septimius Severus in 200 AD, led by Gaius Varro, a seasoned explorer. They sailed north, chasing rumors and legends. And then... nothing. They vanished."

"That's all?"

Palmer nodded. "But don't think that guarantees a supernatural end. Exploring, especially in that time, was a dangerous and frequently fatal endeavor. They could have hit a storm and ended up on the bottom of the ocean. But I suppose anything is possible. If you're interested in the original text, you can find a digital copy of Emperor Severus's journal on the Museum of London's website. It makes for fascinating reading."

Maria stood and held out her hand. "Thank you, Professor. You've given me a lot to think about."

The professor's grip was warm and his smile appeared genuine. "I'm always happy to indulge a curious mind, Ms. Kane. Best of luck in your search."

Maria hurried through the quiet corridors of the history department as she made her way back to the parking lot where her car waited. She hadn't really learned anything groundbreaking, but it seemed clear that the Romans considered Ultima Thule real. Perhaps the explorer had slipped into a pocket dimension somehow and failed to find his way back out.

She shook her head. Though moderately enlightened after her meeting, so much remained a mystery. After supper, she'd take a look at the journal the professor mentioned. She doubted she'd find much, but it couldn't hurt. It wasn't like she had so many leads that she could ignore one.

During the drive home, her mind raced with thoughts of mysterious islands and heaven only knew what might live on them. When she finally pulled into her parking spot, she barely remembered arriving. Talk about a good way to have an accident. She climbed out, yawned, and stretched before making her way to the elevator up to the apartment she shared with her parents.

She pushed through the door and did a double take. Conryu sprawled on the couch, one leg over the arm, watching a baseball game. Of all the things she'd imagined seeing upon arriving home, this hadn't crossed her mind.

"What are you doing here?" She hurried over and hugged him.

"Waiting. The girls are following the kraken, which seems inclined to swim over every inch of the ocean before going wherever it's headed. I have no idea where the Roman ship went, so following up with that is a problem. Until I find a lead to pursue or someone attacks a city, I'm pretty much stuck. How'd your day go?"

She filled him in on what she learned from Professor Palmer. "After dinner, we can look at the document together."

"We could look at it online, or I could take us to London so we can check it out up close and personal. There might be something magical about it. Plus, if Ultima Thule is north of the kingdom, I need to contact Jemma and see if she has any insights."

"Seeing it in person would be great, but it's the middle of the night there. It's probably better to wait until morning when the museum is open."

Conryu shrugged and nodded. "That works too. I'll leave a message at Jemma's office and ask her to meet us there."

"You seem pretty calm," Maria said. "Given everything going on, I thought you'd feel more anxious."

"There aren't any cities on fire, none of my family or friends are in danger, and the Reaper isn't mad at me. All things considered, despite a couple of issues, the world appears in good shape. Since I can't think of anything else to do, I plan to rest and conserve my strength. If there's one thing I've discovered since starting this job, it's that when things go to hell, they tend to go all at once."

Maria didn't have an argument for that, so she asked, "What do you want for dinner?"

CHAPTER 7

Conryu ended up spending the night at Maria's place. While they couldn't take full advantage of that with her parents around, he thoroughly enjoyed the home-cooked dinner. He'd also filled Mr. Kane in on the current situation. As the head of the Department of Infernal Investigations, Conryu had assumed the president would keep him in the loop, but apparently not. No doubt the ongoing election had something to do with it.

He yawned and rolled out of the Kanes' spare bed. Nothing and no one had interrupted his sleep despite having cellphone coverage. It was a good sign for the overall peace of the world, but Conryu didn't trust it for a moment.

A small badge indicated he'd gotten an email. He tapped it and sure enough, Jemma had replied early this morning. The message said she'd meet them in front of the museum at one in the afternoon London time.

"Shit!" That was only half an hour from now. He brushed his teeth, threw on his clothes, and made the short walk down to Maria's room. "Hey, we need to get going."

A few seconds later she opened the door dressed in an oversized T-shirt and squinted, bleary-eyed, hair going every which way. "It's six thirty."

"Yes, and Jemma wants to meet up at one their time. I'm not the best at math, but I'm pretty sure that's only half an hour from now."

"Twenty minutes," Prime added unhelpfully.

"That's not enough time," Maria said.

Conryu concentrated then snapped his fingers. The renewal spell had the effect of a dry shower.

Her eyes widened. "New spell?"

"Sort of. Come on. It feels weird for me to be the one hurrying you."

She glared at him, then shut the door. Fifteen minutes later she emerged, dressed for business in a charcoal pantsuit. Conryu summoned his staff and used it to open the library doors. As soon as they entered, time basically stopped.

Before willing them to London, Conryu said, "Galen."

The ghostly librarian appeared, looking like a translucent Merlin with his long beard and robe. "How may I guide you, Chosen?"

"Do you have any books on Ultima Thule?"

Galen cocked his head for a moment, then said, "No, I'm afraid not. What is it?"

"Either an island the Romans dreamed up or a real island no one can find. That's what we're trying to determine."

Conryu approached the scrying crystal in the center of the room and pictured Jemma. A moment later, he found her standing on the museum steps, dressed in a red Ministry of Magic robe.

An effort of will shifted the library to a discreet location on the right side of the museum entrance, and he opened the door. He and Maria stepped out onto the marble steps and climbed down to join Jemma.

She spotted them at once and waved.

When he reached her, Conryu held out his hand. "Been a while."

"A peaceful while." Jemma shook his hand, then Maria's. "Please tell me you're not here to change that."

"I'm not planning to. Let's go inside. The front steps probably aren't the best place for us to catch up."

"Good point." Jemma led them through the front door.

Inside the museum, only their footsteps and the murmur of voices from hundreds of visitors touring the exhibits broke the quiet. They passed ancient weapons, tarnished medallions, and tomes of all sorts. They were relics of a past age, each with a story, most long forgotten.

"I arranged a room for us. The journal you're interested in should be there already." Jemma turned down an unmarked hall then opened a door labeled "Employees Only."

Not long after, the trio entered a modest square room with only a table and two chairs. In the center of the table lay a tattered journal.

Conryu reached for it, his fingers brushing the cracked spine and brittle cover. No magic or danger lurked inside. As far as he could tell, the only remarkable thing about the book was its age.

Maria leaned in, an eager glint in her eyes. "Can you imagine? A Roman emperor actually held this. How cool is that?"

Conryu smiled. She had always been more into this stuff

than he had. "Why don't you go ahead and read it? I'm sure it's in Latin. Once you're done, you can give us a summary."

"Will do." Maria settled in, Conryu and Jemma already clearly forgotten.

As she pored over the pages, Conryu turned to Jemma. "Let's step outside so she can concentrate."

Once the door closed, Jemma asked, "Do you really think this island is real?"

"Yup. I think there's a demon temple there, and they somehow expanded the pocket dimension to cover the whole island."

"Is that possible?" Jemma asked.

Conryu turned to Prime. "It is, right?"

"Depends on the size of the island," Prime said. "But if it's not huge, then yes, it should be possible."

"And what if you're wrong?" Jemma asked.

Conryu shrugged. "Wouldn't be the first time. I've discovered this job is as much about eliminating the wrong things as finding the right ones. Do you want to join me when I go have a look around?"

Before she could answer, the door opened, and Maria came out looking glum.

"No luck?" Conryu asked.

Maria shook her head. "I confirmed what Professor Palmer told me. It was cool to read something written by an honest-to-goodness Roman emperor, but I didn't find anything especially valuable."

"Well, at least now we won't be wondering. So, what do you say, Jemma? Want to fly north with me?"

"No, I have too much to do as it is. This is one of those rare occasions when I'm not going to wish you luck. The last thing the kingdom needs is a demon temple on our northern border. Whatever you find, I trust you'll keep me updated."

"You bet." He started to summon the library doors when a ninja appeared and took a knee. "What's up?"

"The kraken has finally stopped moving."

"Great. Where did it end up?"

"Five hundred miles off the coast of South America in about a mile of water. It's lying on the ocean floor."

"Do krakens sleep?" Maria asked.

"Hell if I know," Conryu said.

"It's not sleeping, Chosen," the ninja said. "Its eyes are open. I think it's waiting."

"For what?" Maria asked.

"Good question. After I drop you off, I'm going to find out. Jemma, investigating the north is going to have to wait a little longer. But when I go, I'll be sure to let you know what I find out."

Jemma's face twisted in a pained expression, but she nodded. Conryu frequently left people with a similar look on their faces. He sometimes felt bad about it, but these things came with the job.

Now, to see what the oversized squid was up to.

———

Once Conryu had left, Jemma rubbed her eyes. It was only early afternoon and she already needed a nap. Dealing with the young man always had that effect on her. She had so many little problems to handle day in and day out, but whenever he showed up, Jemma knew her life was about to get extra hectic.

She left the museum via a back door and took to the air.

His Majesty had ordered her to brief him as soon as she finished her discussion with Conryu. She doubted he'd like what she had to say, but hopefully, Ultima Thule would remain a legend. With the kingdom finally all the way back to normal after Atlantis's appearance, she wanted to prevent anything that might set them back.

The flight to the royal palace took under a minute. Jemma landed outside the wall and approached the gate on foot. There were wards everywhere, and she didn't want to accidentally trigger one, mainly because she'd be the one forced to reset it.

As she drew near, the ceremonial guards on duty, dressed in archaic plate armor, came to attention. "Welcome, ma'am. We were told to expect your visit. Please go right in."

"Thank you, gentlemen." Jemma nodded to them and strode through the open gate and across the courtyard.

The entire setup had an old-school medieval feel. You'd think the king would want something more modern for his rebuilt home, but he insisted on keeping the traditional look. The Minister of Tourism had been delighted with his decision.

A second, less imposing gate provided access to the main keep. She pushed through the heavy wooden door and stepped into the blessedly modern entry area. A moment of concentration allowed her to confirm that the king was in his office on the second floor. He wore a ring that enabled her to detect his location anywhere he went. Though designed as an anti-kidnapping precaution, it also proved useful in moments like this.

Jemma hurried through the halls, nodding to clerks and government officials as she passed, but never slowing. She'd visited the castle enough times that the setting no longer impressed her, and soon she stood in front of the office door.

She knocked and said, "Majesty, it's Jemma."

"Come in."

The door opened with an unpleasant squeak of metal on metal, intentionally designed to alert the nearby security team that someone had entered the king's office.

And what an office it was—fit for a king, as the saying went. A master carpenter had hand built everything from warm hardwoods. The king's desk featured elaborate carved scenes of dragons battling knights. A bookcase held more decorations than books. Seated behind his desk, the king's smile looked forced. His hair had turned white during the Atlantis incident, and he appeared at least twenty years older than his true age. Jemma really didn't want to add to his stress, but she had to keep him informed about the kingdom's situation.

"Have a seat and tell me what he had to say."

"Yes, Majesty." She settled into a soft leather chair and relayed everything Conryu had told her. When she finished, she added, "It's mostly hearsay, but he seems determined to find out for sure. My fondest wish is that Conryu is wrong about Ultima Thule and that the flying ship he's looking for is far away from here."

The king rubbed his eyes. "Flying ships and krakens, by the Goddess, it's always something. Jemma, I want you to investigate the area yourself. If something's happening, it's our responsibility to address it."

That was the last thing she'd expected him to say. Hesitantly and with the utmost respect, Jemma said, "If there is a demon temple there, responsibility or not, the Ministry can't handle it on our own."

He waved a dismissive hand. "I don't expect you to destroy the place. But if you could scout it out while he's away and let him know what's there, it might be helpful. Given all that he's done for the kingdom, I feel this is a small enough thing for us to do in return."

The kingdom did owe Conryu a great deal, and from his tone, the king was determined that she undertake this task. Seeing no point in arguing, Jemma said, "As you command, Majesty. I'll set out immediately."

"Very good. Best of luck, Jemma."

She stood, bowed, and slipped out of his office. If she was going that far north, she needed to stop by the Ministry to collect a couple of items. Jemma considered gathering a team but dismissed the idea immediately. One person would be far harder to detect than a group.

No, this was a one-person job, and the sooner she finished it, the happier she'd be.

CHAPTER 8

When Conryu arrived at the kraken's location, he opened a viewing portal, and sure enough, found the creature lying on the ocean floor, staring at nothing in particular. He eased back and expanded the portal, but the view didn't get any more interesting. Even with his darkvision spell active, he saw nothing beyond the kraken and the stone of the seabed. He didn't know what else might live this deep, but if anything did, it had wisely relocated.

The whole situation struck him as bizarre. Frowning at the giant squid, he scratched his head and considered his options. Summoning a water spirit to scout might work, but he doubted a spirit would find anything he couldn't see through his portal. He couldn't send the girls in either; they'd be crushed the moment they appeared in the real world.

That left one option. "I'm going to have to go down there and find out what that thing's doing firsthand."

Immediately, Kai said, "I don't think that's wise, Chosen."

Cerberus whined in agreement, and the other ninjas

looked at him with worried expressions. Oddly, Prime seemed to have no negative thoughts on the matter, which was rare when he suggested something potentially foolish.

"Oh, it's definitely not wise." Conryu grinned. "But when has that ever stopped me? The plain truth is, watching this thing from a safe distance is getting us nowhere. If I'm going to do this, better if I do it while the critter is resting. Now wish me luck."

No one spoke as he wrapped himself and Prime in a bubble of water magic. With that done, he transformed his viewing portal into a one-way hell portal and flew out.

The water pressed in on his barrier, but it held easily. The kraken didn't so much as flinch in his direction. It looked like he'd guessed right about it not wanting to fight. Whether it could talk to him or not, time would tell.

"Hello?" He felt utterly ridiculous talking to this thing, but he didn't know what else to try.

Greetings, Chosen of the Reaper. The psychic voice had a gurgly sound in his head.

"Would you be Lord Dagon?"

Indeed. I wondered how long it would take you to figure out that I wished to speak with you. Not as long as I feared, given your limited mortal intellect. Most of your kind see my servant and assume she is a stupid beast seeking only destruction.

Conryu ignored the insult and asked, "If you're not seeking destruction, what do you want?"

I want Narukami Tempest's temple destroyed, his followers slain, and his presence on this world as reduced as my own.

Conryu nodded. He could get down with that plan. The venom in Dagon's voice made his hatred of his rival demon lord clear. Of course, they all hated each other to one degree or another. It seemed to be a feature rather than a bug for all things demonic.

"Was the Roman fellow hurling lightning bolts at your servant a hellpriest?"

No. Narukami Tempest has no hellpriests. What you saw was one of his hellstorm warlocks.

Conryu glanced at Prime. "Would they be similar to Abaddon's hellfire warlocks?"

Dagon answered before Prime had a chance to speak. *They are exactly the same—lesser servants, shadows of a true hellpriest, but a challenge for human wizards all the same.*

Conryu didn't want to get on Dagon's bad side, but one thing gnawed at him. "Why are you telling me all this? Don't you hate the Reaper as much as Narukami Tempest? I assumed you wanted to gain a powerful hold on this world to conquer or destroy it or whatever your particular flavor of evil calls for."

You are mistaken about a great many things, mortal. I hate no being in all of creation more than Narukami Tempest. The arrogant fool thinks he can claim the surface of my oceans simply because he commands the storms above them. It becomes a regular necessity to remind him that isn't the case. I would've eagerly had my servant crush his followers, but they are clever enough to stay out of tentacle range. As for this world, I care nothing for it one way or the other. Destroy Narukami Tempest's followers and I will put my pet back into hibernation for another five thousand years.

This all sounded way too good to be true, but Conryu would happily play along rather than fight two demon lords' servants at the same time. "That sounds like a deal to me. A couple more quick questions and I'll get out of your hair. First off, how do you know Narukami Tempest doesn't have a hellpriest?"

Simple. One of his followers grew disappointed with his station in the cult and stole the temple's core. Without that, no hellpriest can be created, nor can his temple be fully consecrated.

"Do you know where the core is?"

The cultist brought it to me. The core is now safe in the deepest part of the ocean. When all other matters are settled, I will bring it to you so you can destroy it.

That worked for Conryu. The core could wait. "Okay, last question. Where can I find Narukami Tempest's temple?"

There I cannot help you. After the temple core was stolen, the leader of the cult moved it. Where you might find it now, I know not.

Well, that would've been too easy. "I appreciate your help in this matter. You've been much more agreeable than some of the other demon lords I've encountered. No offense, but why is that?"

This world has no sentient underwater species and is thus of no particular interest to me. However, I have encountered several species with the potential to claim this world's oceans once you humans have destroyed yourselves. I am eternal. In time, my followers will claim this world without my having to fight Null for it.

Conryu had no idea whether that was true, but given humanity's destructive tendencies, it was far from impossible. Either way, he'd be long dead before it became an issue.

He offered a polite bow to show his respect to Dagon, not the kraken, which hadn't flinched during the whole conversation. With that done, he slipped back into the borderland and sealed the portal behind him.

"That went better than I feared it might," Conryu said. "What do you think, pal? Will Dagon honor his word?"

"He will for as long as it suits him," Prime said. "His

53

hatred of Narukami Tempest is legendary. Dagon will do anything to see him laid low."

"That's convenient for us. Okay, observation teams, you can head back to the monastery. Tamaki, you're welcome to stay with us or go back to base until a fight looks likely; your call. I need to pop into Black City and ask the boss demon what he thinks about Dagon's offer, then we'll head back to the kingdom and try to find Ultima Thule."

The observation teams both bowed to him and flew off into the darkness. Tamaki hesitated, looking after them for a moment before saying, "I believe I'll stay with you, Chosen."

"Cool. Cerberus, take us to Black City." They flew up onto the demon dog's back and he shot deeper into Hell.

The Reaper must've been eager for the visit since almost no time passed before the sprawling city came into view. Cerberus ran above it, drawing the gazes of the many demons who called the city home. Not that any of them were foolish enough to get in Cerberus's way. The number of demons capable of stopping him were few and the number willing to incur the Reaper's wrath to do so was zero.

At last, they landed in the courtyard of the Reaper's castle, a massive black structure with numerous towers jutting at impossible angles. Black-winged angels circled the fortress on guard duty. Beyond looking cool, he never understood the point of defending the castle given who lived there.

"You guys stay here. I shouldn't be long."

None of them argued. Though the Daughters worshipped the Reaper, they never seemed eager to stand in his presence. If he hadn't known Null would hate it, he would've pitied him. It had to suck to have everyone terrified of you.

"Actually," Prime said. "Having everyone terrified of you is a compliment to a demon lord."

"Of course it is," Conryu muttered under his breath.

A couple of the black-winged angels swooped down for a closer look as he approached the entrance, prompting Conryu to wave to them. The gorgeous female demons smiled back before soaring higher.

The lightest touch made the massive black iron doors swing open. A single stride brought him to the Reaper's throne room. An honor guard of angels lined the path to the throne, where the Reaper's looming presence waited.

"Welcome, my Chosen," Null said.

"Hey. So, I had a chat with Dagon." Conryu filled him in on the discussion. "I'm not sure what to make of his offer, and I wanted to find out what you thought about it."

Null brought a skeletal hand to the dark void outlined by his cowl. "What you describe is very much the sort of deal Dagon would make. At a minimum, you may trust that he won't interfere with your mission to destroy Narukami Tempest's followers. As for the rest, I will speak with him and make a more binding agreement."

"Thank you. I was hoping you'd say that. I don't suppose you could give me any clues about where I might find this hidden temple?"

"No," Null said. "The temple's connection to Narukami Tempest's hell is too weak for me to sense, which is very much a good thing. Find the miserable cowards and wipe them out. They have no place on my Earth."

"Can't argue with you there. I'd best get back. Thanks again for your help."

He barely blinked before finding himself back in the courtyard with Cerberus and the girls. One of the black-winged angels had landed and struck up a conversation with the living Daughters. He recognized Narumi at once.

They fell silent as he approached and bowed as one.

"How did your meeting with the master go?" Narumi asked.

"Smoothly. He seemed to be in a good mood. Since I haven't accomplished much yet, I assume something, somewhere else in the universe is going his way."

"Indeed," Narumi said. "While I don't know all the details, I have heard that he made a new ally on a world that's been troubling him for a millennium or so. The master was most optimistic that he would get good results."

Conryu doubted good results for the Reaper would be good for anyone else, but whatever; it wasn't his world, and he had enough to worry about here. "I hate to cut your visit short, but we need to find that hidden temple."

"Of course," Narumi said. "I was just catching up with the girls since I was between tasks. Best of luck on your hunt."

"I'll take all I can get. Later."

The trio climbed up on Cerberus and then they took off, hopefully to find the entrance to a pocket dimension.

CHAPTER 9

Heather had planned to sleep on her decision about whether to sell her soul to Ardent Lilly. Unfortunately, she hadn't managed more than an hour of fitful rest, so she settled for tossing and turning until midmorning. She rolled out of bed feeling worse than when she lay down and staggered toward the shower.

The handles squeaked when she turned them, the high-pitched noise grating on her already raw nerves. She touched the chilly water and waited. And waited. Fantastic, the hot water was out again. Snarling curses at the asshole landlord, she settled for a cold, quick shower.

Shivering as she dried off, Heather wondered what else could go wrong today. She approached the mirror to dry her hair and grimaced at the bags under her eyes. She wasn't even thirty yet, but today she looked closer to forty. A smoking-hot forty to be sure, but still.

Twenty minutes with the blow dryer and makeup kit helped hide the worst of her bad night. Leaving the bathroom behind, she headed to the kitchen. Since she hadn't been grocery shopping in far too long, her breakfast options were limited to frozen waffles and baking soda. The waffles at least weren't expired, so she popped a couple in the toaster.

This was so pathetic. Heather doubted she had paper to write the contract on.

After her dubious breakfast, she would've sold her soul for a nice medium-rare ribeye and a bottle of Scotch.

Heather didn't know if there was any particular etiquette to writing a demon contract, but she doubted using the back of a takeout menu made the best impression. But search as she might, she failed to find another piece of paper in the entire apartment. Taking a deep breath, she wrote out the terms of the contract, trying her best to remember all the lessons and warnings Mrs. Umbra had worked so hard to drill into their heads during dark magic class. As a water aligned wizard, she hadn't paid especially close attention to those lessons, thinking they'd never be of any use. Not the best idea on her part.

When she finished, all that remained was to seal it with her blood and set it on fire. Did she really want this? No, she wanted her old life back. She wanted to travel the world, party with the rich and famous, and have her picture taken in exotic locales. But an evil, spiteful old woman had banished her from that world. Malice Kincade had taken everything from her after she failed to collect Conryu's genetic material. It wasn't like she hadn't tried. The boy had been too honorable for her own good.

Baring her teeth, Heather grabbed a paring knife and nicked her thumb. When a drop of blood welled up, she pressed it into the contract.

The moment she did, a cold pit formed in the middle of

her chest. Her body felt hollow, as if something that defined her had been ripped away. She knew what it was but didn't want to think too hard about it. Instead, she rolled up the contract and used a spark of fire magic to set it alight. The flames burned a sickly green, consuming the contract in an instant.

When only ashes covered her hand, the cold hollow in her chest filled with black ice. She choked back a scream as she clutched herself.

As quickly as it appeared, the pain vanished, and the now-familiar voice said, *You made the right choice. Practice with your new power; get used to it. When the time comes, you need to be ready to carry out my plan.*

"I will be," Heather said.

Ardent Lilly's amusement came through the new link loud and clear, but she made no comment. Thoughtful for a demon lord.

When the powerful presence had receded to the outer edge of Heather's awareness, she paused to consider her next move. The plan, what little of it she knew, called for Heather to maintain appearances until her new master told her otherwise, but she disliked that idea. The cold shower had been the final straw. Heather needed to upgrade her living arrangements, and she knew exactly how to do it.

CHAPTER 10

Calint's astral form drifted through the ether as he sought the artifact he needed. The ancient weapon had been lost late in the war and certainly forgotten by anyone on this miserable world except for him. How he despised this Earth. Coming here to bring enlightened rule to the primitive humans who called this place home had been the worst decision the High Council ever made, and he was still living with the consequences.

When the surviving elf-bloods made their final retreat to escape Null's demons, he had become separated. By the time he reached the escape portal, the survivors had sealed it to prevent the demons from giving chase, leaving him trapped. The vengeful humans and their demonic allies had done their best to hunt him down, but by dumb luck Calint had stumbled into Narukami Tempest's hidden temple. There, he traded his service and soul for safety and power. It had been a good deal until the term of his master's banishment from Earth ended. Now, his new master expected him to lead his followers in the conquest of this world.

Some days he could hardly stand the déjà vu.

A potent energy source caught his attention and he moved closer, getting near enough to the physical world to see where he was. The weapon sat embedded in the dirt, dormant, waiting for someone who knew how to set it free. A small human settlement had been built around it, but they were of no consequence.

Calint pulled his awareness back. The weapon had ended up on a modest island. Focusing on the portal network, he located the nearest one several hundred miles to the east. It wouldn't take long for the flying ship to make the trip. Gaius could collect the weapon and return in a few hours.

Satisfied with his scouting, he willed his astral body back to his physical form and stood. He'd done this so many times that he didn't so much as wobble when he took a step. Concentrating, he sent a psychic summons to Gaius.

"You should get it yourself," the guardian demon said. "That pathetic human is worthless."

"He's the strongest of the four, and besides, I can't go beyond the temple or fortress. If I do, the Reaper will sense my presence at once. Given his hatred of my people, that would be an instant death sentence."

"As cowardly as ever," the demon said.

Calint didn't take the insult personally. You couldn't really expect much from a demon in terms of personality. They excelled at killing and breaking things, but otherwise he preferred they remain silent and invisible.

The clunk of Gaius's boots on the hard floor arrived half a minute before he did. The human stopped a few feet away and bowed. "Lord Calint?"

"I have located the weapon. Use the fourth rune circle

and head west. There's an island. You'll sense the weapon when you get close. Claim it and return."

Gaius hesitated, seeming uncertain whether he should speak. It was an annoying habit of his. At last, he spat out the question rattling around in his ignorant head. "Why do I not take it and go directly after the kraken?"

"Because the weapon is in a dormant state. It needs to be activated, and I doubt you're capable of doing so, at least not without a year of training. We don't have that sort of time. I expect you back by the end of the day."

"As you command, my lord." Gaius bowed and marched out to begin his mission.

Calint swallowed a sigh. The craftsman in him hated using inferior tools, but he would do his best and hope that conquering this world went more smoothly the second time.

Jemma hung in the air, surveying a vast expanse of nothing. She'd flown north of the Faroe Islands, roughly halfway between Iceland and Norway. The blue of the North Atlantic stretched out as far as she could see in every direction. Though her magical senses had a far shorter range than her sight, they indicated nothing of interest in the area. It would have been convenient to have directions more specific than "north of the kingdom."

But she didn't, so she flew around and hoped for the best. The best in this case was finding nothing, at least in her opinion. Before heading out she'd grabbed two items from the Ministry of Magic's collection: a ring of flight and a ring of invisibility. On long-range scouting missions, both items were essential for conserving her personal magic. If she encountered something dangerous, facing it at less than full power might end with her buried under the waves.

Jemma resolved to cover as much area as possible before dusk, then portal back to London to report to the king.

For now, she focused on the area directly north of the kingdom. Surely, if anything worth mentioning were closer to the other nations, someone would've reported it, even if they weren't part of the Four Nations' Alliance.

A painfully tedious hour passed, and she still hadn't seen anything more interesting than a breaching whale. She stopped to check her phone and a surge ran through the ether.

Jemma spun just in time to watch a swirling portal appear and an ancient, Roman-style sailing ship emerge only twenty yards from her position. She willed herself higher for a better look. Men, at least she thought they were men, from this distance she couldn't say for sure, who looked like extras from a blood-and-sandals epic crowded the benches where rowers would've sat if the ship had possessed oars. They appeared to have period-appropriate weapons, and curved shields rested beside them.

The man standing at the ship's helm crackled with magical power, a mix of wind and dark. That fit with what Conryu had told her about the demon lord they faced. As much as she hated to admit it, something—maybe Ultima Thule, maybe not—was definitely going on around here.

Jemma noted the GPS coordinates on her phone, then fell back to a hopefully safe distance behind the ship. It flew due west, in the general direction of Iceland. What they hoped to find there, she had no idea. Part of her was just glad they weren't heading toward the kingdom. An unworthy thought, but an honest one.

The ship made steady progress toward Iceland. Jemma debated trying to warn them about the approaching threat, but she had no cell signal and didn't know who on the island to call in any case. Some diplomat back home might know how to contact them, but it was a moot point for her.

As they drew closer, clouds gathered, and the sky darkened. The winds picked up and she had to add her own magic to augment the ring's power to keep making progress. Thunder cracked and a bolt of lightning flashed far too close for comfort. Jemma knew the ship's destination. She needed to return home and alert someone before one of those lightning bolts hit her.

She turned to fly away, but another blast of wind struck her square in the face. It hit with such force that she ended up tumbling through the sky out of control.

Not sure which way was up, Jemma did her best to right herself. She also added a Cloak of Darkness, and not a moment too soon. A bolt of lightning slammed into her, sending her cartwheeling through the skies once again.

At least her cloak dissipated the worst of the energy.

"Those who dare spy on Narukami Tempest's great work shall be slain! Their bones shall be left to feed Dagon's fish!"

She followed the voice back to its source and found the helmsman staring at her. Glowing red eyes peeked out from the slits in his bronze helmet. He held a gladius in his right hand, which crackled with lightning.

Jemma dove as he thrust it at her. This time the lightning bolt missed by inches. Its passing made all her hair stand on end.

She kept flying toward the water, only pulling up a few feet above the icy waves.

More lightning rained down.

Jemma wove a random path while praying that his aim from such a distance wouldn't be great.

The lightning stopped and she blew out a breath. That had been far too close.

No sooner had the thought formed when a massive gust of wind hit her with enough force to send her splashing into the ocean. Even through her barrier, the cold struck like a sledgehammer.

Holding her breath, Jemma used her flying spell to propel herself through the water like a torpedo. She also added an aura of heat to keep from freezing to death A shadow passed over her as the ship descended. Looked like her opponent had no intention of letting her escape. Ropes ending in steel grappling hooks splashed all around her as they tried to drag her out of the water.

Jemma concentrated and activated a water-breathing spell. That relieved the pressure on her lungs and she dove deeper, hoping it would be enough to avoid getting hooked.

Escape, on the other hand, looked increasingly unlikely.

———

Gaius kept his ship hovering a foot above the water as he tracked the spy's life force beneath the surface. He didn't know how the woman had found them. This part of the world was supposed to be empty. Just more ill luck. Had he not known the old gods were fiction, he would've thought they'd cursed him.

This was supposed to be a simple mission. Gaius had planned to use it as an opportunity to prove to Lord Calint that he deserved his position, but now some random wizard had ruined it. He'd skin her alive for that.

"Keep throwing those hooks!" he shouted. "Let them sink deeper. She's at least fifteen feet down."

He could've ordered his troops into the water; they were amphibious after all. But he didn't have a good sense of this wizard's strength. If she killed them all, he'd be forced to rely on the first-generation troops, who were far too stupid. Not that his current force would fare any better in a battle of wits.

Gaius loosed a lightning bolt into the water. Not because he imagined it would do any good, but to relieve his frustration. After so many years, they were finally free to act and immediately everything fell apart. All his patience and practice with the powers Narukami Tempest had granted him so far had amounted to nothing.

"Deeper! You're not letting the hooks fall far enough!"

He swallowed a sigh. They were never going to catch her this way.

Gaius took a breath to order the thralls into the water, consequences be damned, when he sensed a powerful presence pass through his storm. He recognized the Reaper's Chosen at once. No one else on the planet, including Lord Calint, had such a potent magical aura.

Suddenly, capturing the wizard interested him a good deal less than escaping. Before he could shift his ship into its ethereal form, a dark-clad figure hit the deck. A book with a demon's face floated at his side.

When the young man met Gaius's gaze, his own death reflected back. With no other options, he resolved to die well.

CHAPTER 11

Conryu emerged from the borderland in the sky above the North Atlantic. When you looked at it on a map, the area didn't seem as vast as it was in reality. The area north of the Kingdom of the Isles covered hundreds of square miles and he could only check a quarter mile at a time. Assuming he didn't get lucky, searching for the pocket dimension was going to take some time.

But you had to do what you had to do. He sent light magic out in every direction, spreading it thin in hopes of covering as much area as possible. Of course, he hit nothing.

Conryu turned to Prime. "I don't suppose you have a spell to speed this up?"

"No, Master. Dark magic is useful for a lot of things, but this isn't one of them. If we get close, I'm certain I'll sense something, but right now all we can do is search."

"I figured you were going to say that."

Chunk by chunk, they searched until an hour had passed with nothing to show for it. Pausing to take a quick break,

Conryu looked around at the empty sky. Talk about the middle of nowhere.

At least the process didn't take much power. He could send out the pulses and maintain his flying spell all day without breaking a sweat. Assuming he didn't fall asleep in midair out of boredom.

What a depressing thought.

He was about to resume the search when something distant and dark tickled the very edge of his perception. "Prime?"

"I sense it too, Master. I'm confident whatever's out there is connected to a different hell than the Reaper's."

This might be the break they'd been looking for. Conryu opened a hell portal and ducked into the borderland.

"Chosen?" Kai said.

"Looks like we're going to get some action after all. Come on." He shifted the group west toward the source of the corruption, using a viewing window to guide them. It didn't take long to spot a huge storm cloud in the otherwise clear sky. "Bingo. I'm going first. You two be ready to jump in. I'd like at least one prisoner if at all possible."

Kai and Tamaki had their swords out and ready. He always found the sight reassuring.

He shifted back to the real world, and powerful winds immediately buffeted him, trying to drive him out of the sky. Ambient corruption ran all through the storm, making it hard to sort out where it came from. As best he could tell, the source was closer to the water.

He wrapped himself and Prime in Cloak of Darkness and dove. A couple of weak lightning bolts fizzled as he passed through the storm, then he spotted the ship. Twenty soldiers in Roman armor were throwing grappling hooks over the side. He couldn't begin to guess what they were after, but if they wanted it, he didn't want them to have it.

The ship looked like the same one that fought the kraken, but he couldn't tell for sure. If the cult had more than one, it spoke volumes about the size of Narukami Tempest's following.

Whatever. It didn't matter. He could sort out the details once they finished the fight.

Conryu hit the deck hard and lashed out with dark magic. All the soldiers' weapons and armor rusted in an instant; all but the one he took to be the leader. His equipment remained intact. The sword crackled with lightning, confirming its enchantment. Hardly a surprise, since nothing else could resist his magic.

"Kill him!" the leader shouted. "Kill the Reaper's Chosen!"

The soldiers surged forward to attack, their eyes glowing with hellish light. They also had oversized mouths filled with rows of razor-sharp teeth. Ugly things but not extremely so, at least as demons went. The monsters had to be some kind of thrall.

A tap of his staff sent a surge of telekinetic force outward, scattering the demons across the deck like blocks slapped by a toddler. Kai and Tamaki appeared, their black iron swords wreaking havoc as the creatures struggled to their feet.

Trusting them to handle the small fry, Conryu focused on the leader. He didn't feel anywhere near as strong as a hell-priest. Must be one of the hellstorm warlocks Dagon mentioned.

As if to prove it, a lightning bolt lanced out from his sword.

Conryu dodged, not trusting Cloak of Darkness to handle a spell cast by a follower of a different demon lord.

He countered with a stream of Divine White Flames. The holy fire burned through whatever protection his opponent had in place and reduced him to ash in an instant. Conryu hadn't even used his full power.

So much for taking him prisoner.

He turned to help the girls, but they had already sliced most of the thralls to chunks of flesh. They darted in and out of the borderland, every blow severing a head or limb.

And just like that, Conryu, Kai, and Tamaki stood alone on deck.

"Pitiful," Tamaki said. "I hoped for more of a challenge."

"Not me," Conryu said. "Too bad I incinerated the only one who might've been able to give us a clue. We'll have to search the ship and hope we can find something useful."

"Master, I sense a human in the water under the ship."

Conryu frowned and sharpened his magical senses. Was that Jemma? What in the world was she doing here?

He leveled the staff and concentrated. A bubble of pure ether formed around her and lifted her onto the deck. Thoroughly soaked and ragged looking, Jemma stared at him as if he might vanish at any moment.

A swirl of mixed fire and wind magic dried her off and made her hair dance around like a medusa. "Better?"

She nodded. "Thank you for the spell and the rescue. I feared they were going to hook me eventually. What are you doing here anyway?"

"I was about to ask you the same thing. I had just started searching for the pocket dimension when I sensed their summoned storm. When I came looking, I found these things fishing for something. I never would've guessed they were after you."

"His Majesty ordered me to scout the area and try to find

Thule for you. He feels a debt for all you've done to help the kingdom. I saw the ship emerge from a portal and followed it. They didn't seem to notice my presence until the storm appeared."

"The hellstorm warlock's awareness was likely connected to the storm," Prime said. "When you passed through the corruption, he must've sensed it."

"More importantly," Conryu said, "did you see what lay beyond the portal?"

Jemma shook her head. "It was all a hazy white space."

That matched how Melina described the barrier surrounding Abaddon's temple. That had to be a good sign. At least Conryu had a good feeling about it.

"I can show you where it appeared," Jemma said. "I noted the exact position on my phone."

"Cool. Is your phone okay?" Conryu asked. "I'm not sure how long you were underwater."

Jemma's eyes widened, and she hastily pulled her phone out of her pocket. She tapped the on switch and blew out a breath. "It's fine. Ministry phones are waterproof, but I was worried the lightning might've fried something. Looks like my protective spell held."

"Great. I want to check below deck, then we can take a look at what you found. Do you want to come with, or would you rather wait up here?"

She looked around at the scattered body parts and grimaced. "I'll come with you."

Conryu didn't blame her. It looked like a demonic funeral home had exploded up here.

As he walked toward the steps to the lower deck, Conryu glanced skyward. The clouds were already breaking up as the sun tried to poke through.

White light burst from the staff's crystal. He sensed nothing dangerous waiting below, but there were ways to hide your presence, and he planned to take nothing for granted. The holy light would weaken any creature of corruption lurking about.

"What is that smell?" Jemma asked when they reached the bottom step.

Conryu shook his head. He'd never visited a place demons called home and found it smelling of roses. The faintly ionized air down here smelled better than some of the places he'd gone.

Where rows of benches for rowers would've been, he found only empty space. There were no crew quarters either.

"Thralls don't need to sleep, Master," Prime said.

"Maybe not, but I have yet to meet someone in charge who didn't want a space for himself. That warlock had to have an office or something."

They kept searching and eventually found a closed door at the rear. No wards protected it, but Conryu disintegrated it with a burst of dark magic just to be safe. Inside, they found an office of sorts. A table and chair faced a small window which offered a nice view of the waves. Sadly it lacked a bookcase or logbook or anything else that might tell them something useful about Ultima Thule or Narukami Tempest's plans.

"Looks like we struck out." Conryu climbed back up on deck. One of the thralls' helmets had rolled into his path and he gave it a kick. The bronze clattered and tumbled across the deck until the head inside rolled out. "What the hell?"

He hurried over for a closer look. The dead thrall vaguely resembled a human, but it had gray skin to go with its pointed ears and serrated teeth. Conryu had never seen anything like it.

"Why haven't they started dissolving?" he asked.

"I'm not certain, Master. Perhaps they're not thralls after all but some new creation."

"Swell, a new flavor of evil. Just what we need."

CHAPTER 12

Conryu flew east alongside Jemma, who had her phone out to guide them to where she'd seen the portal appear. He'd left the enemy ship drifting in the borderland, marked with an ethereal tag that would allow him to find it when he figured out what to do with the cursed thing.

"What confused me," Jemma said, "was why they were headed for Iceland. I haven't heard anything about demon activity in the area. We don't have the closest relations with them, but I'm confident that if something serious happened the diplomatic corps would let me know."

"What makes you so certain they were going to Iceland?" Conryu asked.

"I mean, they were headed right for it."

"Yeah, but with a flying ship obscured by magic, they could've flown right over the island and continued to who knows where. Iceland wasn't necessarily their target."

Jemma considered for a moment. "You might be right. Given their route, I jumped to conclusions."

"I'll station a team in the area," Conryu said. "If another ship shows up, they'll let me know."

"I find that very reassuring. We're getting close." Jemma slowed, then came to a stop and pointed to a spot on her right. "This is it. The ship emerged right there."

Conryu released a wave of light magic, but it hit nothing. He sensed no lingering magical residue. "What do you think, pal?"

"I sense nothing, Master," Prime said. "This section of sky is the same as every other section we checked."

"Yeah, that's the impression I get too." He wanted to shout and curse but held it in. Losing his temper would accomplish nothing. "I'm starting to think we have the wrong idea about Ultima Thule. The problem is, I have no idea what the right idea might be."

"If the Ministry of Magic can be of any help," Jemma said, "don't hesitate to contact me. For now, I need to update His Majesty."

"Sure, thanks for the help. Stay safe."

Jemma waved and soared back toward the kingdom.

Once she had gone, he rubbed the bridge of his nose. Another dead end. He'd been so sure he'd find something out here. On the plus side, as long as Dagon had the temple core, Narukami Tempest couldn't create a hellpriest. While the hellstorm warlocks were formidable, they paled in comparison to a proper hellpriest.

"I think it's time to bring in our research expert." Conryu tried his phone but, of course, had no signal.

He marked the portal location with an ethereal beacon and returned to the borderland. The girls were waiting with Cerberus. All three looked at him with patient expressions.

He often wished he had as much faith in himself as they had in him.

"Tamaki, do me a favor and run back to the ship and grab one of those monster heads. I want Narumi to look at it."

She bowed. "Yes, Chosen."

While she was gone, he concentrated on the former leader of the Daughters of the Reaper. "Narumi, could you join me for a moment?"

Hopefully, the Reaper hadn't found something more important for her to do. A little while later, a bright spot approached from deeper in Hell. It soon resolved into the black-winged figure of Narumi.

When she reached them, she wrapped her wings around her body and bowed. "How may I be of service, Chosen?"

"We ran into some weird, demonic... things. I've never seen anything like them and Prime said he hadn't either. I thought you might have some insight."

"I'm happy to take a look, though if your scholomantic doesn't recognize them, the chances that I will are pretty low."

Prime's pleasure at the compliment radiated through their link, drawing a smile from Conryu. His familiar did enjoy getting his ego stroked.

Tamaki returned as their conversation was winding down, the severed head in her hands. She held it out, and Conryu nodded toward Narumi, who took it. She examined it closely, going so far as opening the mouth for a better look at its teeth.

When she got to the base of its severed neck, Narumi frowned and said, "Look, Chosen, just above the cut. There are two more slits. They look rather like gills."

He moved closer. They certainly did look like gills.

Amphibious assault troops was the first thing that came to mind. "Prime, how did we miss those?"

Prime grumbled but didn't comment, drawing a grin from Conryu. "So, do you know what they are?"

Narumi shook her head. "I can sense a bit of lingering corruption in it, but this creature certainly isn't a demon. More like a corrupted human. Well, not exactly human, but you know what I mean."

He did understand what she meant, more or less. "How tough would you say these things are?"

"They're weak and pathetic," Tamaki said. "I can't imagine why any demon lord would bother with such sad creatures."

"I was thinking more about how they'd fare in really deep water. Could they withstand the pressure a few miles down?"

Narumi let out a little sigh. "I wish I could tell you, Chosen, but I have no experience with things like this. The best advice I can offer is to assume the worst."

"Why does that worry you, Chosen?" Kai asked.

"Well, when I look at these things, all I can think is that someone wants a way to retrieve Narukami Tempest's temple core. I know where Dagon is hiding it, and these things look like they were designed to try and reclaim it. If there are more of them and they succeed, we're going to have a problem."

"Those weaklings wouldn't last a second against the kraken," Tamaki said.

"They don't have to beat the kraken. If a boatload of them dive at once, only one needs to get lucky, grab the core, and flee while the others keep the kraken busy. Just to be on the safe side, I need to warn Dagon."

Traveling through the borderland, it took only seconds for Conryu to reach the Challenger Deep, the deepest part of the ocean. The kraken lay on the ocean floor, seeming untroubled by the immense pressure. He'd half expected to find the creature beset by a force of those shark-looking things.

This part of the ocean was miles deeper than the last place he emerged and despite his considerable magical power, Conryu had no intention of testing his barrier against the crushing force of so much water. As he'd often been told, with magic, pretty much anything was possible. That being the case, he should be able to modify his viewing portal to allow sound and thoughts to pass through.

First, he moved as close to the real world as possible. He got so close that time ran at the same rate on either side of the portal. Now came the tricky bit. Focusing all his will on what he wanted, Conryu said, "Narukami Tempest appears to have aquatic troops at his disposal. I don't know if they're strong enough to descend this deep, but I wanted to warn you."

His imitation monsters don't worry me. I've dealt with them on many other worlds. Though you have only seen one of my servants, rest assured I have others. The temple core has been safe here for thousands of years and will continue to be safe until you fulfill your end of the bargain.

Conryu nodded, somewhat reassured. "Have you and the Reaper sorted out the details of your arrangement?"

Fragments of our awarenesses are hashing the matter out as we speak. Negotiations will not be difficult. I care little for this world, and Null is more reasonable than most of our fellows.

Since they were talking about demon lords, Conryu wasn't sure how big of a compliment that was, but he kept the thought to himself. "I'll resume my search then. Good afternoon."

He closed the portal. Dagon sounded confident. Of course, all demon lords were confident. When you were omnipotent and immortal, it was no doubt hard not to be. For all their sakes, his confidence had best not be misplaced.

———

C alint sensed it immediately when the useless excuse for a warlock died. Their connection through their shared service to Narukami Tempest made his death echo like a ringing bell in Calint's mind. He stood and paced around the chapel. Gaius hadn't been terribly impressive, but he should have been sufficient to deal with a village of powerless humans.

In fact, a handful of Calint's amphibious assault troops would've been enough to deal with them. Since Gaius got himself killed, it meant the troops had been killed as well. What a waste of the most advanced of his creations. The earlier batches were adequate despite their stupidity, but only just.

Losing the flying ship, on the other hand, was a bigger problem. They had only one, and Calint had to assume it ended up in the hands of whoever killed Gaius. Now he had no undetectable way to move his troops. All in all, the mission couldn't have gone much worse.

"Whoever killed him?" the guardian demon said. "I think we both know who is most likely responsible: the Reaper's Chosen."

Calint finally released the sigh he'd been holding in. "Indeed, your assumption makes sense, but we have no proof. Not that it matters; Gaius will be no less dead regardless of who killed him. Perhaps I should've sent one of the others."

"The other three are more worthless. Send me to retrieve the weapon. If that fool of a wizard shows up, I'll rip his head off and send his soul to his master."

Calint raised an eyebrow at that. "Will you now? Given the number of guardian demons the human has faced and defeated, most in their own temples, where they're strongest, how do you imagine you'll accomplish this feat?"

"Don't compare me to those weaklings. No human, no matter how strong, is a match for me, regardless of where we fight."

Calint shook his head at the demon's familiar arrogance. Sending him wasn't the worst idea; in fact, given the nonexistent alternatives, he had little choice but to send the demon or abandon the quest for the weapon.

"Very well, I'll send you. We'll need to loosen the bindings holding you to the temple first, but that's a simple process."

"Then begin! I haven't rent mortal flesh in far too long."

"As you wish." Calint raised his hand and gathered corrupt ether.

A moment later, the demon howled in pain. "What... are... you... doing?!"

"Loosening your bindings. I said the process was simple, not painless. Now keep quiet, I have to concentrate."

Calint kept his amusement hidden, but he found the demon's pain delightful. If it had been a long time since the demon had torn the flesh of mortals, no doubt even more time had passed since it felt true pain.

These little reminders served an important purpose, not least to remind the demon who was the master here.

CHAPTER 13

Maria was back at her desk, tapping away at her keyboard in the vain hope of finding anything useful about Ultima Thule. It had been cool to read the emperor's journal in London, but ultimately, the text proved worthless as anything beyond a historical footnote. Sadly, the internet didn't offer up anything of greater value.

She closed a tab and rubbed her eyes. Researching legendary historical places and events was exhausting. Maybe a quick lunch would fire her up.

Halfway to her feet, someone knocked from behind her. She spun around just in time to see Conryu emerge from the door to the library. "Hey, got a minute?"

"Sure, I was just getting ready to take a break. What's going on?"

"I ran into that ship again. The crew has been dealt with and I thought you might be able to learn something useful if you had a firsthand sample to work with. Does the Department have a warehouse or something where I could put it?"

Maria stared silently for a moment. "You captured the enemy ship? Does that mean the threat is over?"

"I did capture a ship, but no, the threat isn't over. It won't be until I find and purify the temple and destroy the guardian demon. I'm still working on that part. I'm not sure if it's a good thing or a bad thing, but as far as I can tell, there's no pocket dimension north of the kingdom."

"But that's where all the legends say Ultima Thule is."

"I know, but it's not there. We did find a portal, sort of. If the last group of explorers accidentally passed through it, that would explain how they vanished. Anyway, that's all speculation. What about the warehouse?"

"I have no idea. Let's go ask Dad. If anyone can point us in the right direction, he can."

Maria led the way out of her office and down the hall to her father's office. His secretary looked up from whatever she was working on and frowned. She always frowned when Conryu showed up. It no longer bothered him, but Maria still got annoyed on his behalf. Considering all he'd done for the world, people should be more grateful.

"Is Dad free?" Maria asked.

"One moment." She pressed the intercom and said, "Your daughter and Mr. Koda are here, sir."

"Send them right in."

Still glowering, she motioned them toward the door. When they entered Dad's office, he got up from behind his desk. He wore his usual fine gray suit. His bald head shone in the office's lights. Some of the dark smudges were gone from under his eyes, and he seemed less stressed than usual, which came as a relief to Maria.

A good chunk of Central City was visible through the windows. The skyscrapers gleamed in the bright sunlight.

Maria wished she had such a nice view from her office, not that she'd have time to enjoy it.

"Conryu, sweetheart, what brings you two by?" Maria got a hug and Conryu got a handshake. "Have a seat and tell me how I can help."

Conryu brought him up to date, beginning with the president's call and ending with the battle against the hellstorm warlock and whatever his minions were. "So I need somewhere to store the ship so we can study it. Those weird shark-looking monsters are still aboard, so if you have a biologist on staff who can take a look, that would be helpful as well."

"As usual, you've been busy." Dad scratched his chin. "We have a research facility that should serve. How big is the ship?"

"I have no idea. Kai, could you measure it for me?"

A couple of minutes later, a disembodied voice said, "Sixty paces long and twenty wide, Chosen."

"That should fit no problem." Dad reached for his phone. "Let me call the research director and make sure they have room for it. They're always working on something. Since you're acting on the president's direct orders, I'm confident they'll find space for you. Hold on."

Maria leaned closer and whispered, "I'm quite excited to see an ancient Roman ship in person. Lately, it's been like we're living in a history class."

"Don't get too excited. Whoever built it made a bunch of changes. Turns out flying ships don't have much use for oars, so those are missing along with the sails. For some reason, they kept the mast."

"Maybe so the lookout has somewhere to watch from," Maria said.

He nodded. "Maybe."

"Thank you, Professor." Mr. Kane hung up. "They've got a spot for your ship. How soon can you bring it in?"

"Ten seconds. It's floating in the borderland just waiting to be delivered. If you've got an address for me, I can drop it off right now."

Dad jotted down an address and handed Conryu the sheet of notepaper. "You two should drive over first and introduce yourselves before you show up with an enchanted ship. I told Professor Marchand to expect you, but be sure to take your official identification."

Maria smiled. "I never visit a Department facility without it."

Conryu stood and shook Dad's hand again. "I appreciate the help, sir."

"Happy to do it, son. That's what I'm here for after all."

Conryu and Maria left her dad's office and headed for hers to grab her purse. Once she had it, they made their way to the parking lot and Maria's car. Conryu sighed as he slid into the passenger side.

"What was that big sigh about?"

"Just thinking about how long it's been since I took my bike for a spin," Conryu said as she pulled out of the parking space. "I miss it. Also, why is your dad being so helpful all of a sudden? Usually, he wants something from me."

"A government-wide memo went out this morning, direct from the president's office. You're to get whatever help you need, whenever you need it, no questions asked. Failure to comply is a fireable offense."

"That's handy. I should've threatened to introduce the president to the Reaper when this chaos began. It would've saved me all sorts of trouble."

Maria hated the bitterness in his tone, not that she didn't understand it. Given all that he'd done for the people of the world, he'd been treated rather poorly by many of them. Lucky for everyone he didn't let his feelings keep him from doing the right thing.

The drive to the warehouse only took ten minutes and soon Maria was parking in front of a set of huge double doors. Above them, someone had welded a smaller version of the Department's black pentagram symbol.

"I think this is the same industrial park where the Academy picks up supplies," Conryu said. "I arrived on the opposite side when I came through. I wonder if the Department owns the entire park."

Maria had never been here before, and despite her father's high position in the Department, she had no real idea how many facilities they had scattered around, not to mention whatever black sites Malice had set up before her death.

They got out, and Maria marched over to the little door on the side of the warehouse. As she walked, she pulled her laminated ID card out of her purse. When she knocked on the door, a slot opened, and a pair of suspicious eyes peered out.

"This is a secure government facility," the owner of the eyes said. "Please back away."

Maria held up her card. "I work for the Department. Dr. Marchand should be expecting us."

The eyes narrowed, then shifted to Conryu. "Where's your ID?"

"Unlike Maria, I don't work for the Department. I'm just here to help with the delivery."

Maria wanted to giggle when Conryu imitated the tone

of the guy who delivered a rug to their apartment during a visit a couple of years ago. He sounded so bland it was funny.

"I'm not sure I can let someone in without an ID."

"Tell whoever's in charge of this tin shack that Conryu Koda is here to drop off a flying Roman ship and unless they want me to leave it out here, they'd best let me in."

"Give me a second." The slot slammed shut and Maria could just hear the patter of footsteps.

"Guess he didn't read the memo," Conryu said.

Maria smiled and took his hand. "He's probably a minimum-wage rent-a-cop whose only joy in life is hassling people who show up without an ID. Once he tells Dr. Marchand we're here, he'll be lucky if he has a job tomorrow, so why not go easy on him?"

"Yeah, I know. I'm just a bit frustrated. Finding Narukami Tempest's temple is proving trickier than I expected. I should be used to it by now, but every job hits the same way: find clues, hit dead ends, and repeat until you find the target and purify it. It would be nice to skip some of the middle and go right to the end, but sadly it never works out that way."

Two sets of footsteps approaching ended the conversation. Instead of the slot opening, the whole door did. Inside, a stern woman with short hair, round glasses, and a white lab coat over a business suit stood beside a decidedly nervous-looking man in a guard uniform. The guy couldn't have been more than a year or two older than them.

"I'm Dr. Marchand," the woman said. "I apologize for the misunderstanding. Please come in. Should I order the main doors opened?"

"No need," Conryu said. "I'll bring it right through by portal. Just show me where you want it."

"I've arranged a gantry to support the ship. Follow me."

Maria and Conryu fell in behind her and walked through the warehouse.

Maria had been expecting a typical collection of loaded pallets stacked to the ceiling. Instead, it looked more like a research facility. People dressed like Dr. Marchand were busy working on what looked like tanks and cars equipped with cannons on one side. The other side was open, and a set of heavy steel pillars mounted on tracks had been set up about thirty feet apart.

Dr. Marchand led them to the gantry. "If you could put the ship between them, I can adjust the width to support it."

"Sure," Conryu said. "But it doesn't need supporting. The ship flies. I'll bring it in about six inches above the floor, and it'll stay there—level—unless you move it. I'm not sure what sort of magic is used to control the way it flies, but maybe you can sort that out."

"Fascinating. We can just use the gantry lift to reach the deck. I can't wait to discover what sort of magic allows something the size of a Roman ship to fly."

Conryu summoned his staff, and Maria's heart skipped a beat when he pointed it at her. A moment later, a bubble of light magic formed around her.

She understood the precaution when he opened a hell portal bigger than any she'd ever seen in front of the gantry.

Conryu loosed a piercing whistle then said, "Cerberus, push it through."

Foot by foot, the massive wooden vessel emerged. Seeing it in person was much more impressive than hearing Conryu's description. From the little gasp beside her, Dr. Marchand was equally impressed. All around the warehouse, everyone had stopped what they were doing to stare at the slowly emerging ship.

When the rear end of the ship appeared, Maria caught a glimpse of Cerberus's three heads before they pulled back and Conryu shut the portal. He sighed with relief and dissolved the protective bubble around her.

"You okay?" he asked. "I knew a portal that size would give you trouble if I didn't take precautions."

"I'm fine. Didn't feel a thing, thanks. That ship is really something."

"It certainly is," Dr. Marchand said. "I can't wait to study the mechanism they used to make something that big fly. The energy required must be immense."

"The main thing you need to focus on is where it came from," Conryu said. "Any hints about the source of the wood or magic or anything will help me find the people I need to deal with. Also, there are about twenty bodies on deck. I don't know if you have biologists here, but anything you can tell me about them would be helpful as well."

"Bodies?!" Dr. Marchand said.

"Yes, but only one of them is human—well, mostly human —and that one's now little more than ash. I'm not sure if you still qualify after you sell your soul to a demon lord. Anyway, as soon as you learn anything useful, have one of Maria's bodyguards contact me. Actually, Tamaki, would you head back to the monastery and get me Linna's squad?"

A few seconds later, four black-clad ninjas were kneeling in front of Conryu. No matter how many times Maria saw them do that, she still couldn't quite believe it was really happening.

"How may we serve, Chosen?" asked one of them—Linna, Maria assumed.

"I'm assigning your team to guard this warehouse and serve as messengers for Dr. Marchand. They'll be investigating the flying ship for me. I need to know as soon as they learn anything. Okay?"

"Understood, Chosen. We will guard this building and the people inside with our lives."

Conryu shook his head, a little exasperated smile playing around his lips. "No, you are not to get yourselves killed. If something you can't handle pops up, come find me or call for reinforcements."

"As you say, Chosen." The ninjas stood and bowed before fading away.

"There you go. There's no faster way to reach me than ninja mail. Soon as you learn anything, ask for Linna, and she'll let me know. Though I'm not optimistic, I'm going to see what I can figure out on my own." Conryu kissed Maria on the cheek. "Later."

He summoned the library doors and disappeared, leaving Maria alone with Dr. Marchand. The older woman rubbed her hands together and said, "Shall we begin?"

CHAPTER 14

Heather pulled into her usual parking spot behind the club. She longed never to visit the miserable place again, or better yet, watch it burn to the ground. Ardent Lilly's dark power whirled through Heather's body, intoxicating and repulsive at the same time. A disturbing emptiness reverberated in her core where her soul used to reside. Or so she assumed. Having never traded her soul before she couldn't know for sure.

She forced the unsettling thoughts aside. She'd made her choice, now she had to live with it.

Leaving the parking lot, she made the short walk to the club's entrance. Barely a step inside, a sticky patch on the floor made a disgusting squelching sound as she raised her foot. The stale air smelled of sweat, beer, and other unsavory odors she preferred not to think about. The pounding music hurt her ears.

Disgust twisted her lips. Heaven's mercy, she hated this place.

Heather rushed along the back corridor toward her

dressing room and nearly collided with her frowning boss in the cramped passage. The slob wore his shirt half unbuttoned, exposing a flabby chest covered with oily black hair and gold chains.

"Where have you been?" His chins wobbled as he shouted. "I should dock your pay."

Heather smirked. "Have you found someone to replace me as your headliner?"

His beady eyes narrowed. "Bitch. Hurry up and get ready."

"I'd be ready now if you hadn't gotten in my way." Heather pushed past him into her dressing room.

"Ten minutes!" he shouted after her. "Or you're done here!"

She slammed the door on his empty threat. Firing her would be a mercy. Soon enough she wouldn't need this dump. That day couldn't come soon enough.

Heather shimmied into her skimpiest sequined costume. It didn't have enough pieces for a long set, but the men didn't care. The faster she got naked, the happier they'd be. She swiped on some crimson lipstick and called it good. The MC called her name and the crowd roared.

Showtime.

Leaving her dressing room, she resolved never to set foot in this dump again. This performance would be her final show and damn the consequences. Heather squared her shoulders and strutted onstage.

The pounding beat vibrated in her bones as she prowled across the stage, her hips swaying seductively. Despite her halfhearted effort, hungry eyes followed her every move. She looked them over in turn. Typically, Heather disregarded the crowd, but tonight she had other plans.

Three-quarters of the way through her performance, she noticed him. Lounging in a corner booth, oozing wealth and arrogance, Heather recalled his chiseled features from tabloid photos. Derek something or other, a recently divorced real estate tycoon. The headline had labeled him a billionaire. Heather labeled him the perfect target.

He glanced in her direction and Heather fixed her gaze on him. She flung her top his way before twirling around the pole. When she popped in to say hi later, she expected a warm welcome.

As the music ended, Heather blew a kiss to the audience and sauntered offstage amid raucous cheers and obscene catcalls. She returned to her dressing room and changed into her street clothes. Even a pair of jeans and a blouse transformed into designer fashion when she wore them.

Heather stared at her reflection then focused on her new power. Her eyes burned for a moment before glowing red. Good. She released her focus and let the glow fade.

Now to see about upgrading her living quarters. Heather left her dressing room, and rather than slip out the door, she made her way toward her target's booth.

He smiled as she settled onto the cushion opposite him and held up her top. "I think you lost this."

She shook her head. "It's club property. You can leave it on the table with your tip."

"Do you think the owner would mind if I kept it as a souvenir?"

Their gazes locked, and Heather activated her new power. His features slackened as the domination spell took control.

Heather stood and curled a finger. "Let's go to your place now."

Derek got to his feet and she grasped his hand, pulling him through the hooting crowd and out into the parking lot. She snatched his keys from his grasp and smirked as she pressed the key fob. A sleek red sports car flashed its lights. Heather's smile broadened. It had to be a million to one odds that he'd have the make of car she used to drive, only a couple years newer.

Maybe fate really had smiled on her when Ardent Lilly entered her life.

Settling behind the wheel, she pressed the ignition and the engine roared to life. The familiar vibration made her feel like her old self for the first time in a long time.

She turned to the puppet beside her. "Where do you live?"

He rattled off the address of a luxury development she would've lived in back in the day.

She pulled out of the parking lot and sped across the city, reveling in the sensation of driving a real car again. Heather didn't worry about leaving her old car behind. No self-respecting thief would bother with the worthless thing.

The drive ended far too soon and before she knew it her mindless companion directed her to his reserved parking spot beneath a sleek high-rise. A nearby elevator whisked them up to the penthouse. Heather grinned as he unlocked the door, which opened to reveal a sprawling space defined by clean lines and floor-to-ceiling windows that overlooked a twinkling skyline.

She belonged here, not in that dingy little apartment across town.

Heather forced Derek onto the leather sofa. He lay there with his gaze fixed on nothing in particular. Her magic had reduced him to little more than a living, breathing husk, though she sensed that if she desired, he would perform any task she wished no matter how repulsive or risky.

She eased into a plush leather armchair across from him and rested her heels on the glass coffee table. Crystal decanters arranged on the wet bar across the room caught her attention. A drink would suit her perfectly.

She snapped her fingers. "Prepare me a drink: a vodka martini with three olives."

Derek jolted up, then shuffled to the bar. He executed the task smoothly, looking for all the world like a regular person. Good, if he couldn't pass for normal, he'd be useless should she require his company.

Heather accepted the drink while surveying her new domain. Gleaming hardwood covered the floors and tasteful modern art hung on the walls. She couldn't have designed a more perfect home.

Derek remained motionless, his gaze fixed into empty space. No spark of life flickered behind his glazed eyes after he carried out her command. Sharing a drink with a zombie killed some of her high.

A shudder ran through her and she set the glass down with a sharp clink. While the power intoxicated her, these hollow shells, both his and hers, reminded Heather of the steep price she'd paid.

Driven by a powerful urge to escape her involuntary companion, she made her way toward the bathroom. Maybe the hot water would wash away the dirty feeling.

Ardent Lilly's mocking laughter echoed in her mind. *Don't tell me you are getting weak in the knees already, we've only just begun.*

Heather gritted her teeth. "I am not weak. I'm just getting used to my new circumstances."

Good. You would do well to settle into your role as soon as possible. The president will be in town for a fundraiser tomorrow. You're going to seduce him, get him on video in a... compromising position. Then he'll lure Conryu into our trap. Assuming he doesn't want his wife and the media to find out about his affair with former model Heather James.

Heather smiled. The idea of controlling one of the most powerful people in the world pleased her no end.

"And how will this trap work?"

One thing at a time. First you need to secure our patsy. Once you're ready, I'll share the next stage.

The corrupt presence vanished and Heather continued on her way to the bathroom. The sooner she washed away the psychic sludge, the better.

CHAPTER 15

C onryu emerged from a hell portal in Reykjavik, specifically in an empty alley downtown. He still doubted the Roman ship planned to attack Iceland, but with no better options until Maria figured out where the ship came from, he figured it couldn't hurt to have a look around and see what he could learn.

Somewhere in the distance, a siren wailed. Sounded like someone else was having a bad day.

Conryu strode out of the alley. Before he arrived, he'd looked up the address of the city's largest museum on his phone. The empty alley where he appeared was only a couple of blocks away. The midafternoon sun shone down from a bright, clear sky, and plenty of people wandered the streets, all of them tall, blond, and fit. Conryu's half-Japanese features stood out like a sore thumb, though no one paid him much attention aside from a couple of double takes.

Soon, he spotted the stone front of the National Museum of Iceland. It stood tall and imposing, with walls made of gray rock. Its large, arched window frames featured intricate carvings of Viking runes and symbols, none of them actually enchanted.

A few people came and went, so he joined the flow. The inside didn't differ much from the London Museum; the displays just had a Viking theme instead of a knightly one.

Conryu moved silently through the exhibits, scanning each as he passed for anything that might indicate whether Narukami Tempest had any interest in this place. Prime floated invisible and silent beside him. Strangers often reacted poorly the first time they met Prime, and he wanted to avoid any drama.

He passed displays of Viking-age weapons, their blades still looking sharp enough to draw blood, and fragile manuscripts illuminated in vivid colors. A collection of strange talismans carved from stone and bone caught his eye, but they held neither the spark of ether nor the darkness of corruption.

Three-quarters of the way through the museum, the familiar feeling of a wild-goose chase struck him. Then he spotted a display on Norse gods, dominated by a large painting of a muscular man with red hair wielding a hammer that crackled with lightning.

Conryu stared at the painting. Thor, the Norse god of thunder and lightning. The similarities to Narukami Tempest were too obvious to ignore. He couldn't believe he'd never considered the connection until now.

He leaned in closer, scanning the placard. Most of it covered the usual mythological fluff, but one line caught his eye: "Legend holds that Thor's hammer, Mjolnir, fell to Earth long ago, landing in Iceland."

Conryu's pulse quickened. This had to be what Narukami Tempest's forces had targeted.

You're jumping to conclusions.

Prime had a point, but he planned to check it out anyway. They even provided an address where the supposed magical hammer hit.

Bet it's a tourist trap.

Maybe, but Conryu couldn't ignore the possibility of finding something important. He committed the historical site's location to memory, turned, and strode out of the museum.

Outside, he grabbed his phone and searched for the address. It was about half an hour outside the city, in the mountains—half an hour by car, that is. Conryu had quicker ways to travel.

He found an out-of-the-way spot and entered the borderland. Using a viewing portal to guide him, he flew along the road leading to the supposedly magical hammer. Kai, Tamaki, and Cerberus floated silently beside him, waiting for orders.

If he'd had the time, this would've made for a nice ride. The rugged Icelandic countryside looked stunning in the afternoon light. Craggy black stones dotted with stubborn patches of greenery stretched out on either side of the road. He made a mental note to bring Maria here during their next break; they could take his bike for a ride and have a picnic.

The pleasant fantasy vanished when he spotted a little village. Moving closer, he approached the edge of the buildings, where a fenced-in area contained a shining metal warhammer, carved with runes and half embedded in the ground. A modest shop sat to one side of the clearing, and maybe twenty people milled around, getting their pictures taken with the hammer and generally looking things over. He couldn't say what he expected other than something else.

Conryu exited the borderland just outside the village and walked in, heading straight toward the clearing. Ignoring the tourists, he approached a middle-aged woman in a park ranger uniform who stood nearby, keeping an eye on the goings-on. As he got closer, he activated a translation spell.

"Quite a sight, isn't it?" The ranger smiled when Conryu got close. "The legendary hammer of Thor himself."

Her tone held a faintly amused note, clearly indicating she didn't take the legend very seriously. Conryu nodded and watched as a burly man with a red beard tried unsuccessfully to lift the hammer.

"Has anyone ever succeeded in picking it up?"

The ranger laughed. "Plenty have tried over the centuries. We have quite a tradition of strong men in this country, and they all come here at least once to try, but it hasn't budged an inch. Legend says only one worthy of the power of Thor can lift it."

"Is that so?" The crowd had cleared out enough for him to approach. "Is it okay if I give it a whirl?"

She shrugged, clearly amused at the idea of a skinny little guy like Conryu lifting it. Given the size of the last guy to try, he didn't blame her for her skepticism. "Everyone's welcome to try; just don't be too disappointed when it doesn't move."

He eased closer, circling the half-buried hammer. Whoever made the thing had etched runes along the handle and around the head. But not Viking runes, though they looked vaguely familiar. Even without touching it, Conryu sensed the weapon's potent magic, but thankfully it remained untainted by corruption.

They're elf runes, Master.

He did a double take. This thing's an elf artifact?

I believe so, Master. Though what it does, I can't say.

Why would followers of Narukami Tempest want an elf artifact? Likely for the same reason everyone wanted one: the power they held.

Before Conryu could attempt to lift the hammer, the sky darkened far too quickly for a natural storm. Ominous clouds streaked with lightning swirled overhead. The hairs on the back of his neck stood on end as corrupt energy crackled through the air.

"Everyone, take cover!" Conryu waved at the crowd.

People screamed when a massive figure plummeted from the eye of the storm. Shiny black plates covered its body and bat wings sprouted from its back as lightning writhed across it in jagged bolts.

The demon slammed into the earth with a thunderous impact, sending clods of dirt and rock spraying. It had to stand at least eight feet tall, with the glowing red eyes typical of its kind. Given the power it radiated, this had to be the temple guardian. If he could destroy it, that would deliver a significant blow to the enemy.

The demon's eyes glowed brighter as they locked onto Conryu. "My master will be well pleased when I kill you, Reaper's Chosen."

Its voice grated on Conryu's ears, and its corrupt presence made him feel queasy. He summoned his staff and commanded the crystal to blaze with Divine White Flames. "Bring it on."

Tamaki appeared behind the demon and slashed her black iron blade across its back. As soon as the edge made contact, lightning arced into her body, making her shudder and spasm for an instant before the magic blew her across the clearing and through the shop wall. Hopefully all the crashes and crunches were breaking boards, not bones.

Much as he wanted to, Conryu couldn't take the time to check on her now.

Instead, he hurled a blast of white flame. The spell drove the demon back a step without causing any real damage. As he'd expected, this thing was no pushover.

It countered with a bolt of lightning, and the battle began.

Explosions rocked the clearing as they darted around, neither able to gain the advantage.

The demon roared, lightning gathered around its clawed fists, and it charged.

Conryu tapped the ground, and hands of dense earth shot up to grab the demon's ankles, sending it sprawling in the dirt.

Before it could recover, he hit it with a focused blast of white flames.

It howled in pain and fury as its whole body sizzled and burned away. A powerful jerk of its leg freed it from the earthen grasp, and a moment later, lashing its wings, it took to the sky.

For a moment, he thought the demon might flee. Then he noticed the tornado slowly descending from the black clouds. A twister that big would wipe out the entire village.

He couldn't allow it. Switching from white flames to dark magic, he conjured a concentrated ball and hurled it at the approaching tornado. His spell tore apart the magic holding the funnel cloud together, dissipating it with a final gust.

The demon roared in frustration but didn't descend for another round. Instead, the clouds slowly broke up. When it cleared, the demon had vanished.

Conryu hadn't truly expected it to stick around for a final showdown. He had hoped, but in vain.

When it became clear that the fight was over, for now, he hurried to check on Tamaki, who lay in a heap of broken boards. He sent light magic into her, healing broken bones and soothing burned skin until she fully recovered.

Kai appeared beside him. "I tried to warn her, Chosen."

"Don't worry about it." He tapped Tamaki gently on the cheek. "Hey, talk to me. Are you okay now?"

She groaned, her eyelids fluttering open. "Chosen? I thought its back was wide open. What happened?"

"I drove it off for now. Can you stand?" He held out a hand and helped her to her feet.

"Forgive me, Chosen. I shouldn't have rushed in until I better understood what the demon could do. The other creatures were so weak; I assumed this thing would be as well."

"We all make mistakes. I'm confident you won't make that one again." He gave her a quick hug. "I'm glad you're alright."

When he let her go, Tamaki faded back into the borderland, followed by Kai.

With the immediate threat dealt with, he turned his focus back to the hammer. As long as it remained here, these people would remain in danger. While he doubted they'd thank him for stealing something of such cultural significance, it seemed a small price to pay to avoid future demon visits.

Conryu probed the hammer with tendrils of ether and found a spell connecting it to the ground. That explained why no one could move it. A stream of dark magic shattered the binding, and he picked the weapon up without issue.

Time to split before anything else nasty showed up, like an angry park warden. He summoned the library doors, and the girls appeared beside him before all three of them stepped inside. Once the doors closed, Conryu walked to the rear of the library, where a large table covered with elf artifacts waited. He added the hammer to the collection and frowned.

"Prime, can demons use elf artifacts?"

"I can't imagine why they wouldn't be able to, Master. And even if the demon couldn't use it himself, a hellstorm warlock wouldn't have any trouble, assuming he knew how."

Conryu rubbed his eyes. Well, they'd stopped the enemy from gaining a potent weapon at least. It didn't feel as satisfying as killing the guardian demon, but for now, it would do.

———

C alint's thin, bloodless lips quirked up in a faint smile when he sensed the guardian demon's approach. The creature had only been gone for half an hour, so he assumed it had been successful. A good result in general, though it would no doubt increase the demon's already near-insufferable arrogance. He considered that a price well worth paying to claim the weapon.

As the demon got closer, his smile turned down. He couldn't sense the weapon at all. Despite its dormant state it gave off tremendous energy. Calint should be able to at least detect some trace of it at this range. Apparently, he'd been too quick to give the demon credit for success.

He turned to face the black stone altar and a moment later the demon entered the chapel via an opening in the ceiling. It landed facing him across the altar. Lines ran through its carapace and some of the fine edges had been melted dull. All in all, it looked like it had taken a bath in molten lava.

"Where is the weapon?" Calint asked.

The demon loosed a little growl and flexed its claws. "Still in Iceland, stuck in the dirt where it landed."

Calint cocked his head. "And why is that? You should've had no trouble disengaging the lockdown spell holding it there. Was my explanation of the process insufficient in some way?"

"I never got a chance to try and free the weapon. The Reaper's Chosen had already arrived."

"Why was that a problem?" Calint asked, his tone innocent. "Surely you slew him easily. I looked forward to displaying his severed head above the temple entrance."

"He was stronger than I anticipated. We fought and he forced me to flee." The last three words came out as a mumble.

"I'm sorry, you were what?"

"He drove me off! Are you satisfied, wizard? I couldn't beat him. The flames of Heaven did this to me!" The demon gestured at his damaged exterior. "I could feel them burning away my very essence. Never in my eternal existence have I experienced such a thing. The pain was unimaginable."

"I see." Calint forced himself not to rub it in despite his earlier warning about the enemy's power. "Well, this is certainly a disappointing turn of events. Without the weapon, given our current resources, we have no way of defeating the kraken and claiming the temple core."

"The master will not be pleased," the demon said. "Surely there's some other way."

Calint tapped his chin and paced around the chapel. He had at his disposal fifty or so first-generation amphibious troops and three more hellstorm warlocks, all of them weaker and stupider than the late Gaius. Together they still wouldn't be enough to make a difference in battle with the Reaper's Chosen even if he sent the demon along as well.

No, violence would only lead to failure. He needed to find another way around this problem and he needed to find it before the Reaper's Chosen found them.

CHAPTER 16

Maria stared at the warlock's armor lying on the blood-stained deck. Conryu had reduced his body to little more than ash, but the armor had come through reasonably intact. She appreciated the lack of a body. The warlock's human appearance gave her the creeps. Demonic things should look the part.

She shuddered and put the unpleasant thought out of her mind.

Around her, Department workers in coveralls hauled away the mangled corpses of the demonic creatures littering the deck. Those had been killed by ninja swords and were still very much intact and, from the smell, beginning to rot. Whoever said being a wizard wasn't a glamorous line of work knew what they were talking about.

Right, focus. They needed to find out whatever they could to help Conryu locate Narukami Tempest's temple. Surely there were some useful clues amidst all this unpleasantness.

Professor Marchand knelt beside the warlock's armor,

inspecting it with a critical eye. "This is strange," she muttered. "The craftsmanship is exquisite. But look, this steel is far too advanced for ancient Rome. It looks like modern metal."

Maria frowned. "Why would anyone make old-style armor out of modern steel? There are so many more practical sorts of protection if that's what they were worried about."

The professor shook her head. "I don't know. Perhaps we'll find some clues below deck."

Leaving the grisly mess behind, they descended the steps to the second level and found it largely empty. Maria didn't know if those monsters slept, but if they had to, they did so huddled on the deck without so much as a blanket.

She and Professor Marchand went to the warlock's cabin next. They found it nearly as empty as the rest of the second level. He had a simple table and a chair. Apparently, the warlock didn't need to sleep either since he didn't have so much as a hammock. At least no stench lingered in the air. In this line of work, you had to take what you could get.

"Maybe there's something hidden." Professor Marchand sounded as dubious as Maria felt. Nevertheless, the two women got busy searching.

Maria ran her fingers along the walls, reaching out with tendrils of magic to probe for any hidden compartments. After a few minutes without success, she moved on to the floor, where she found exactly the same thing, nothing.

"This is a bust," Maria said. "Let's try the lowest level."

"Good idea, though I have little hope given what we've found so far." Professor Marchand blew out a long sigh. "I think these people, assuming that's the right word, take security very seriously. They left nothing behind that might lead an enemy to their hiding place."

"Let's hope they weren't as thorough as you think."

The hold was their last chance, but as Maria climbed down the final ladder, a sinking feeling settled in her gut. A conjured light revealed more empty space; just bare wooden planks and stale air. She scanned every corner with narrowed eyes and probing magic but found nothing.

"I don't understand," Maria said. "What were those creatures on deck planning to eat? There're no food stores."

Professor Marchand rubbed her chin. "Demonic creatures often require no food to survive."

"Or maybe they weren't planning a long journey." Maria's mind raced. "If they were only going on a quick strike before heading home, that would explain the lack of supplies."

Of course it was all guesswork. With more questions than answers, they climbed back to the top deck. At least the workers had finished clearing the bodies out of the way. Maria had no desire to look at them for a moment longer than necessary.

"I'm quite curious about the magic that enables this vessel to fly," Professor Marchand said.

Maria nodded. "It's the only thing we haven't checked yet. I'll start in the front."

"That leaves the back for me." Professor Marchand strode toward the rear of the ship.

Putting the older woman out of her mind, Maria lost herself in magical analysis. It soon became apparent that the magic had no single source. She'd assumed an artifact in the helm handled the flight magic, but no, she found the energy evenly distributed through the entire hull.

The style felt familiar, but she couldn't quite put her

finger on where she'd seen it before. She kept working, turning it over in her mind as she went along.

When the answer came, she cursed herself for missing something so painfully obvious. The magic felt just like an elf artifact. But she'd never heard of one this big before. Few people knew about her research into the artifacts and she hesitated to tell Professor Marchand, but at the end of the day, keeping secrets would only hold them back.

"Professor, the magic is identical to an elf artifact."

The professor's eyebrows shot up. "You have experience studying elf artifacts?"

"A bit, but that's not the point." She hastened to shift the focus of the conversation away from her. "How did human demon worshippers learn to create elf artifacts? As far as I know, nobody has ever managed to duplicate one."

Professor Marchand moved to stand beside Maria in the center of the ship. "That's my understanding as well. Given their power, this could be a major threat."

"Hello!" The shout from below jolted Maria out of her thoughts. She and Professor Marchand peered over the railing to find one of the scientists waving at them.

"I found something, Professor!" the man said.

Maria and the professor exchanged a glance before climbing down to the warehouse floor. The scientist hurried over to meet them. The young man looked about Maria's age. He wore thick glasses and a lab coat and practically vibrated with excitement.

"I've identified the wood the ship is made of," he said. "It's iroko, a hardwood native to Africa. Preliminary analysis indicates it was cut in the last fifty years or so."

Maria stared, certain she must've misheard. "Africa? Are you sure?"

The scientist nodded. "One hundred percent. It's unmistakable."

He droned on about pore structures and parenchyma cells, but Maria stopped listening. No human had called Africa home since before the elves arrived and mutated the local wildlife, turning the continent into a death trap. How had the cult of Narukami Tempest ended up there? And more importantly, how had the Romans?

Maria stiffened when the reality hit her. "That's it! The cult must've found an elf ruin and learned how to use their magic. Where in Africa does that wood grow?"

The scientist frowned. "According to my research, the most likely place is the Congo River Basin, but iroko does grow elsewhere on the continent."

"That's fine, it's a place to start. Linna."

The ninja immediately appeared and took a knee. "How may I serve?"

"I have a message for Conryu. Tell him it looks like the target is in Africa, likely in the Congo River Basin. Warn him that we're pretty sure there's an elf ruin involved."

Linna stood and bowed. "I will deliver your message."

And with that she vanished again, leaving Maria with nothing to do but worry.

———

With Thor's hammer, or whatever the artifact really was, secure in his library, Conryu guided them back to London. Once he found a quiet spot in a park, he stepped out into the real world along with the girls, who promptly vanished into the borderland.

He dug out his phone, settled on a handy bench, and

called Jemma. He hoped to catch her before she went home for the night. Since the sun hadn't set all the way yet, he thought he had a pretty good chance.

She answered after two rings. "Conryu, what news?"

"You were right about Iceland. That was their target." He filled her in on the demon's attack. "The damn thing got away, but without the artifact. I'm not sure if that's a win, but at least it's not a loss."

A moment of silence passed before she said, "You fought a demon for possession of Thor's hammer then left with it yourself? None of the locals objected?"

"The locals were all too terrified of the demon to come out of their houses, much less hassle me. I'd be surprised if they've come out yet. Narukami Tempest's guardian demon was nothing to sneeze at."

"That hammer is a historical relic with great cultural significance. You can't just take it."

"Sure I can. Trust me, it's better that I have it than leaving it for the cult to grab. If I left it there, how long before the demon returned for a second try? I doubt it would've gone as well if I wasn't there."

Her sigh sounded utterly exhausted. "I suppose you're right. May I see it?"

"Sure, maybe you'll be able to tell what it does. I haven't a clue. I'll meet you outside the Ministry building."

"Alright, I'm on my way."

Conryu ended the call and opened the library door. Before entering he said, "You two can wait in the borderland. This shouldn't take long."

With that, he entered the library. Since he had no desire to show Jemma his collection of artifacts, he grabbed the hammer then pictured a wall appearing in front of the table holding his collection. It shimmered into place and he nodded. Good, the fewer people who knew about those items, the better.

He went to the crystal ball and guided the library to a spot near the Ministry of Magic's stairs. Once he'd positioned the library where he wanted it, he willed time to flow normally.

A minute later Jemma strode out the door.

He made the door visible and opened it. She started then hurried inside. Once they were securely outside of time, he held the hammer out to her. "What do you think?"

"It's lighter than I'd expect for its size. Given the amount of ether packed inside it's a wonder sparks aren't shooting out of it. No, I take that back, the real wonder is that while I can tell it's powerful, I have no idea what it does or how the energy flows."

"Right? Ever wonder why elf artifacts are like that? I've never seen one that was easy to use."

"Why would the elves make it easier for their enemies to use their weapons?" she asked.

"That's fair, I guess." Conryu shrugged. "Doesn't matter to me either way, as long as Narukami Tempest's followers don't get their hands on it."

"Maybe I should hold on to it for you."

Conryu snorted a laugh. "Do you have a more secure location than an unreachable enchanted library?"

"Good point. Is there any chance I can convince you to return the hammer to Iceland once this matter is settled?"

"No, but I can make a duplicate with a basic enchantment which will make it impossible to lift. Would that work?"

"I guess it'll have to," Jemma said. "I need to return to the office."

He opened the door and stepped out with her. Before Conryu could say goodbye, a ninja appeared and took a knee. Not Kai or Tamaki then.

"What's up?" he asked.

"Chosen, I have a message from Maria. She says the ship appears to be an elf artifact and that it was made with wood found in Africa, specifically the Congo River Basin. She also wishes to caution you that it's likely the cult has found an elf ruin and claimed its magic."

"Well, Maria's been busy too. Outstanding, thank you. Please return and thank her and the rest of the team for their quick work."

She straightened and bowed. "Yes, Chosen."

With that she vanished.

Conryu turned to Jemma, who appeared dumbstruck. A perfectly understandable reaction to the news. When she regained her faculties she said, "How could anyone, even members of a demon cult, survive in that nightmare place? The Congo River Basin is really close to where the elves originally appeared and the danger of visiting the area reflects that."

"Has the kingdom sent expeditions there?"

"Heaven's mercy, no. But private groups have made the attempt and none have returned. I mean, zero people came back alive. Just keep that in mind."

"I will, but if that's where the temple is, dangerous or not, I have to go."

"Then all I can do is wish you good luck." She gave him a nod and headed back to the Ministry building.

Conryu shifted to the borderland and said, "Tamaki, go get Kanna and the others not on another mission. I think this is going to be an all-hands-on-deck job."

Tamaki flew away and quickly vanished from sight. Once she was on her way back to the monastery, Conryu let his mind drift. He had a lot of the pieces to the puzzle, but far too many remained missing. He hoped those missing details didn't end up getting any of his people killed.

It didn't take long for Tamaki to return with Kanna and the other girls. As soon as they arrived, everyone bowed and Kanna asked, "How may we serve, Chosen?"

"Looks like Narukami Tempest's temple is somewhere in Africa, likely hidden in a pocket dimension. My theory is that they're cutting logs in the real world and bringing them back for use in building their ships. Maria gave us a rough target area, but it's still huge. I'm going to need all of you to spread out and search for any signs of human activity, trees being harvested, anything that suggests intelligent beings are behind it."

"And if we find something?" Kanna asked.

"Come get me. Africa is now the most dangerous place in the world, and in addition to mutated beasts we've got demons to worry about. Caution is the word of the day."

"Understood," Kanna said. "Where do you wish us to begin?"

"According to Maria, the Congo River Basin is the most likely source of the trees they're using. That's hundreds of square miles of the roughest terrain you're likely to find, so search as much as you can from the borderland. I'll shift us to the center of the basin and you can spread out from there."

Kanna nodded. "If this isn't going to be a combat mission, I'll have the teams break up into pairs to cover more ground."

"Good idea. Everyone gather around." When the ninjas had moved to surround him, Conryu shifted the whole group to a spot near the center of Africa.

He opened a viewing portal and found nothing but thick, dense jungle in every direction. At this point maps didn't mean much nor did national boundaries, but he felt pretty sure he'd brought them to the right general area.

"This is the best I can do," he said. "Kanna, send your teams out."

Kanna got to work and soon only Conryu, Kai, Cerberus, and Prime were left in their particular section of darkness. Conryu swallowed a sigh. He hated waiting.

CHAPTER 17

Kanna flew slowly through the borderland, her full attention on the dense jungle just beyond Hell's edge. Searching this area was incredibly tedious. If you didn't take care you could easily miss something vital hiding behind a broad leaf. You had to check every inch and the process tested her considerable patience.

Out of the corner of her eye, Kanna caught a glimpse of Tamaki's deep frown. Always one of the most serious of the Daughters, something had been off since Kanna arrived. It was one of the reasons she insisted on pairing with Tamaki for this mission.

"What's troubling you?" Kanna asked.

"Nothing, Grandmaster," Tamaki said.

Kanna stopped and turned to face her subordinate. "If you don't wish to speak of it, that's your choice, but do not insult me again by claiming that nothing is wrong."

Tamaki winced. "Apologies, Grandmaster. Since the battle with the elf, I've felt off. I always considered myself the best warrior in the Daughters, but the elf easily defeated me.

Then when the demon appeared in Iceland, I rushed into battle like a new recruit fresh out of training. I've never been so disgusted with myself. Yet despite my repeated failures, the Chosen hasn't so much as chastised me."

Tamaki hesitated to continue so Kanna waited. The search was important, but getting Tamaki's head on straight took priority. She could afford the time, especially here where time meant nothing.

Taking a deep breath, Tamaki continued. "He healed my wounds and hugged me. I thought after the battle he would ask for someone better, or at least less foolish, to take my place, but he showed no sign of displeasure. I'm not sure what to think, but I know with absolute certainty that I don't want to fail him again."

Kanna glided over beside Tamaki and put a hand on her shoulder. "From the day you began your training, everything has come naturally to you. Your raw talent combined with a willingness to work hard made you the best, but it also denied you the setbacks that most of us face early in our service. And now that you've finally hit a rough patch, you're struggling with how to proceed. Does that sound correct?"

"Yes, Grandmaster, exactly correct. What must I do?"

Tamaki's desperation tugged a bit at Kanna's heartstrings, but sadly she had no easy answers for the young woman. "You must do what you've been doing—your best. Remember the mistakes you made and learn from them. Have the same faith in yourself that the Chosen has in you. If he didn't believe you could stand at his side, rest assured, he would've asked for someone else."

"I will try my best, Grandmaster." Tamaki bowed.

"That's all any of us can do. Now, let us resume the search."

And so, yard by yard, they studied the jungle. Despite being in the dark emptiness of Hell, the dense foliage seemed to close in around them as the broad leaves and tangled vines obscured their view. Kanna narrowed her eyes, scanning the shadows between the trees for any hint of movement or irregularity.

A flash of iridescent blue caught Kanna's eye. She held up a hand, signaling Tamaki to halt. Together they hovered, watching as an enormous butterfly, easily a foot across, flitted between the branches. Its wings shimmered with an otherworldly luminescence.

Kanna had never seen such a creature and couldn't help wondering what sort of dangerous abilities it had. Probably just as well if they didn't find out.

The pair pressed on, passing a stagnant pool of standing water where a chitinous insectoid creature drank its fill. Its head snapped up and multifaceted eyes focused on something nearby. Kanna shifted her position and watched as a sinuous shape slithered down the trunk of a tree into view. The snake's emerald scales glittered in the filtered light and three wedge-shaped heads watched every direction. It glared at the insect creature before vanishing into the undergrowth.

Kanna shuddered. So many horrors in such a short space. This land was like a different sort of hell. It defied belief that even demon worshippers could survive in such a place. With a little shake of her head, she willed herself along. Though interesting, Kanna had more important work to do than study the local wildlife.

Kanna had no idea how much time passed before she sensed someone approaching. It only took a moment to spot a faint light in the darkness. The light resolved into one of the other Daughters. Much as she hated to admit it, Kanna couldn't always distinguish them from each other from a distance.

"Grandmaster." When she spoke, Kanna recognized Mei's voice. After bowing, she continued. "Kami and I discovered signs of logging in our sector. Three huge trees were cut off by a saw. We didn't emerge to confirm how old the stumps are, but we thought it likely this is what the Chosen wished us to find."

"You might be right,' Kanna said. "Show me."

Mei turned back the way she'd come. "This way."

Kanna glanced at Tamaki. "Keep searching this area. I'll be in touch."

"Yes, Grandmaster." Tamaki's tone showed no hint of her earlier doubts. Good.

Kanna followed Mei through the darkness and soon they reached a waiting Daughter, who bowed when she saw Kanna.

A quick look into the real world confirmed the stumps, but she couldn't tell where the logs were taken. If any great amount of time had passed, the jungle would've hidden the paths.

Still, this was definitely a promising start. She concentrated and said, "Squads three, four, and five, to me. Tamaki, you too."

Less than a minute later twelve Daughters and Tamaki had joined her. They stared, silently waiting for orders.

"We've found signs of activity. Spread out from here and search the area. Look for any signs of passage that might lead us to the temple. Tamaki, go tell the Chosen."

———

Conryu wasn't sure how long he'd been floating in the dark, but when he sensed Tamaki returning it came as a great relief.

She stopped in front of him and bowed. "Chosen, one of the teams found signs of logging. Grandmaster Kanna requested I inform you and guide you back to the site. She has already redeployed three teams to search the immediate area."

"Outstanding, I feared it would take way longer to find something. Lead the way."

Conryu, Kai, and Cerberus followed Tamaki through the darkness. Soon enough they reached Kanna, who stood silently waiting.

She bowed when he arrived. "Here, Chosen."

He opened a viewing portal and after a couple micro adjustments had a smoothly cut off stump centered. It had to be better than two feet across, more than enough to make a keel. So where did they take the log?

He checked left and right but saw no trail. Hardly a surprise given how fast the plants grew around here. "I'm going to have to take a firsthand look. You three keep your eyes peeled for anything dangerous heading my way."

He knew he didn't have to warn them, those three were the most reliable of all the Daughters, but still, it never hurt and especially not in a place like this.

Conryu opened a hell portal and entered the jungle. The humid air clung to his skin as he breathed in the earthy scent of the jungle. It reminded him of walking into a greenhouse.

"I was wrong, Master," Prime said. "There is a place worse than Heaven. My pages are liable to mildew."

"You're a demon, I doubt mildew would dare form on your pages. I'm not sensing any magic. How about you?"

"No, Master. Everything feels as normal as possible in this elf-cursed place."

Conryu ran his fingers over the smooth, somewhat slimy surface of the cut. Whoever felled the tree did so years or more likely decades ago. No obvious trail revealed itself.

Just to be sure, he sent out a pulse of light magic, but as expected he found no pocket dimension within range. No one would be stupid enough to harvest a tree right next door to their hidden base, even if that base had been built in the world's most inhospitable terrain.

"Maybe we can spot something from above," he muttered.

Conryu willed himself skyward and soon was looking down on the sprawling expanse of canopy. Nothing but more green plus a little fog in every direction. It might not have been quite as good as the bottom of the ocean, but if you wanted to hide something, this wasn't a terrible second option.

He flew around with no particular destination in mind Conryu had found that sometimes the best way to find something wasn't to look so hard for it. If you let your mind relax and your eyes defocus, sometimes the things which didn't fit would pop out.

A screech from above and to his right made him flinch. Conryu spun and leveled his staff at a twisted monstrosity as it came swooping out of the clouds. It had leathery wings, an ugly, furry body, and a writhing mass of tentacles sprouting from its mouth. Bulbous eyes glared at Conryu from between the gaps in the squirming appendages.

At least the eyes weren't glowing red, which suggested a lack of demonic corruption.

Conryu took all this in at a glance before loosing a blast

of dark magic that reduced the creature to bones and scraps of skin that crashed to the jungle.

He could see how such things could cause normal explorers no end of trouble, but for him they were barely a nuisance. The interruption of his search annoyed him more than the attack itself.

The brief interaction had gotten him out of position. Which sections of jungle had he searched? He muttered curses at elf-made monsters and looked around. He immediately caught sight of a flash of light from running water. Was there a river down there? If the cultists didn't want to leave a trail, moving logs by river would be an option.

He flew toward the water for a better look. Conryu skimmed along a few feet above the choppy surface as he followed it through the dense jungle. It looked deep enough to float a pretty good-sized log.

As he rounded a bend in the river, he slowed. Someone had disturbed the bank. Cautiously, every sense alert for a potential threat, he approached the marks. It looked like something heavy had been dragged away.

Conryu landed in the mud and grimaced as he sank in up to the ankles. As he swiped a hand across his brow to wipe away the sweat, he studied the nearby jungle. He had no trouble spotting where they entered the trees. Given the size of the logs and the difficulty of the terrain, he couldn't imagine they'd want to drag them very far.

A pulse of light magic confirmed that there were no pocket dimensions within range. He debated shifting back to the borderland, but you lost so much detail using a viewing portal. No, he'd continue in the real world, heat and humidity be damned.

Conryu flew above the mud as he followed deep furrows

left by the dragged logs. The trail wound through dense undergrowth. Vines and creepers snagged his clothes as he pushed through the foliage. Moderately annoyed, he expanded his light magic barrier out a few inches; that would keep anything from getting through.

"You could always rot a path through using dark magic," Prime said.

Conryu nodded toward a collection of brilliantly colored flowers in vivid shades of crimson, violet and orange growing from the bark of a tree. "And ruin all this? I don't think so. Despite the danger, this area is still beautiful. There's no point in destroying it."

Prime grumbled something but Conryu ignored him. If Prime ever stopped complaining, then he'd start to worry.

The drag marks swerved around massive tree trunks and went over gnarled roots jutting from the ground. He couldn't imagine what they used to move the logs through this mess, but it had to be powerful.

About a quarter mile down the path, the jungle began to change. The dense undergrowth thinned, eventually opening up into a clearing. Gnarled trees with trunks as wide as houses running all around the perimeter bent together in the middle, their branches intertwining overhead into a dense weave that blocked out the sun. No tree ever grew like that naturally.

Bioluminescent fungi clung to the bark, bathing the forest floor in an eerie blue glow. The sounds of the jungle grew muted, replaced by an odd hum that vibrated deep in his chest. Conryu had never felt anything like it and he didn't know what to think.

In the center of the clearing, a steel elf ruin waited. Unlike the one in Central America, nobody had built a stone demon temple above this one. The structure measured easily ten times the size of the first ruin he visited and the skid path led right to it. There were four windowless metal towers connected by a high wall surrounding another tower that reached nearly to the canopy.

Though not at all optimistic, Conryu checked with light magic. As he expected, he found no pocket dimension. He did find a barrier protecting the elf ruin.

"What do you make of it, pal?"

"Elf magic is difficult to analyze," Prime said. "But my guess is that the barrier serves as a stealth field to keep enemies from locating this place magically. That would've come in handy during the war."

"Yeah, I bet whoever lives here never imagined someone just following a trail back to them."

"Given the number of people living on this continent and the jungle's reputation, the odds of discovery hardly bear considering."

"Fair point. I don't sense any corruption. Do you think the barrier is blocking it?"

"Possibly, but I can't imagine Narukami Tempest building a temple here. It doesn't feel like the sort of place his followers would choose."

"Well, one way to find out for sure. Kai, Tamaki, Kanna." The ninjas appeared and he continued. "I don't know what we're walking into, so just in case something in the elf ruin interferes with your abilities, I want you in the real world when I approach."

"We are with you, Chosen," Kanna said.

She and Kai moved to his right side while Tamaki took his left. Ready as he'd ever be, Conryu set out for the ruin.

CHAPTER 18

P resident Vincent Langston stood in front of the mirror in his hotel suite, his reflection a portrait of exhaustion. His eyes were dark and bloodshot from lack of sleep, and his hair, while not falling out, yet, had turned mostly white. Some days he wondered why he was so eager for another term. If the other side wanted to try and keep a country of half a billion people safe and prosperous, maybe he should give them the chance.

He blew out a breath and adjusted his bow tie. He preferred his gray suit, but this fundraiser was a formal event, making the tuxedo a necessity.

As he fussed in the mirror, his mind wandered to the evening ahead. The fundraiser, the endless handshakes and forced smiles, the pressure to secure campaign funds, it came with the job regardless of how much he hated it.

Vincent's shoulders sagged. If only Melissa had been able to join him. The presence of his dear wife always steadied him. Her gentle temper and keen wit did wonders to pick him up. But tonight he faced the crowd alone. Melissa remained in Central to host a three-day conference on women's issues.

A knock on the door pulled Vincent out of his thoughts.

"Mr. President, it's time," the muffled voice of his lead security agent said.

After a final tug at his bow tie, Vincent straightened, the familiar mask of confidence slipping into place. Time for this monkey to dance.

As he strode toward the door, his thoughts turned to Conryu. He'd heard nothing from the young man for two days. Not long enough to concern him, yet he couldn't help wondering what happened to the kraken and flying ship. He shook his head. Neither of them had attacked the Alliance and in the end nothing else mattered.

He pulled the door open and stepped into the hallway. His security detail fell into formation around him, a phalanx of suits and earpieces, as they made their way toward the ballroom. No one spoke on the elevator down. When the doors slid open, one of the agents muttered something into his microphone before nodding and motioning the group out.

The ballroom waited only a few yards down another hall. The murmur of conversation mixed with clinking glasses and the soft music of a string quartet. Crystal chandeliers cast a dazzling glow across the sea of designer gowns and tailored tuxedos, the opulence of the room serving as a testament to the wealth and influence of those gathered. The campaign had already raised over half a million dollars from this event with no doubt more checks to come later.

The crowd fell silent once they finally noticed his arrival. Every pair of eyes turned his way. All the attention used to bother him, but he'd long since gotten used to it.

Someone started clapping then a full-on cheer erupted. They all wanted something from him. Eventually they'd let him know what they imagined their money had bought. As long as they kept the requests reasonable, he might let them have what they wanted.

Vincent raised a hand, waving to the assembled guests, his smile practiced and hollow. Steeling himself, he stepped into the fray. He moved through the crowd, shaking hands and exchanging pleasantries, the picture of a charismatic leader, or so he hoped The faces became a blur as he went from one bland comment to the next.

Eventually, desperately in need of a break, he extracted himself from the sweaty grasp of a software executive and made his way toward the bar.

As soon as he arrived, the bartender, a dark-skinned fellow in a tux with the sleeves rolled up to display his muscular forearms, hurried over to take his order. "Sir?"

"Scotch, neat."

The bartender promptly poured and delivered his drink. As he lifted the glass to his lips, a flash of movement caught his eye. A woman, her presence overwhelming, glided through the crowd, her gaze fixed on him. Something about her tugged at his mind, but damned if he could place her.

Her long blond hair seemed to blow on an unseen breeze as she approached. The neckline of her red dress plunged to just short of indecent. He'd never seen anyone so strikingly beautiful, outside of his wife. Hopefully some overly ambitious constituent hadn't hired her to entertain him. That happened more often than you might think and it always left him with a bit of an upset stomach.

"Mr. President." Her voice oozed sex appeal, which meant it matched the rest of her perfectly. "A pleasure to meet you."

Vincent's brow furrowed. "Forgive me. Unlikely as it seems, I can't remember your name."

The smile which had been playing at the corners of her lips twisted. "I get that a lot. My name is Heather, sir."

The name rang no bells, yet he felt certain he should know her. The memory danced right at the edge of his mind, but he couldn't grasp it.

"What brings you here tonight, Heather? If it was a donation, I'm most grateful for your support."

Her eyes flashed red.

Vincent's mind went blank. The chatter of the ballroom faded to a distant hum and the world around him blurred at the edges. He blinked, trying to clear his vision, but the sensation only intensified, as if time itself had slowed to a crawl, each second stretching into an eternity.

As soon as it appeared, the feeling passed. He rubbed his eyes and looked around, but Heather had vanished. For a moment he feared he had a stroke, but he immediately shook the thought away. It had to be the stress getting to him.

He turned back to the bar and polished off his drink in a single swallow. The burn of the alcohol sliding down his throat brought him back to reality.

Vincent spun slowly around, his gaze scanning the crowd for any sign of her red dress. And he found nothing. He ran a hand over his face and signaled the bartender, who hastened to approach.

"Sir?"

"Another, please."

As the bartender poured, Vincent asked, "The woman I was speaking to. She seemed familiar, yet I couldn't think where I knew her from. Did you recognize her?"

The bartender offered a nervous laugh and set the tumbler back in front of Vincent. "You're kidding, right, sir?"

"I assure you I am not."

"She was none other than the formerly world famous model Heather James. My younger brother kept her poster on the ceiling above his bed. He said she was the stuff that dreams were made of."

Vincent took a sip of his drink and smiled. "Was your brother a fan of old movies as well?"

The bartender started. "Yeah, how did you know?"

"I recognized the quote. It's from an old detective movie. Heather James, that's a name I haven't heard in a while. What in the world is she doing here?"

"Sir?" the bartender asked.

Vincent shook his head. "Nothing, just talking to myself."

He finished his drink, stood, and straightened his shoulders. Time to get back to his constituents.

———

Heather left the befuddled president at the bar and lost herself in the crowd as she worked her way toward the door. Hardly anyone recognized her. A convenient thing for the mission but a kick to her ego. It hadn't been that long since the peak of her fame and now she'd been forgotten, just another face in the crowd.

Just went to show you how fickle fame could be.

She reached the entrance to the ballroom and slipped outside. The agents on duty shot her a look, but all men did that and she sensed no suspicion in their gazes, only the usual lust.

Once she'd moved out of everyone's view, a faint smirk

quirked her lips. The so-called leader of the free world had fallen prey to her new magic as easily as Derek. Pathetic, but what could you expect from normal men? At least she'd completed the first step in Ardent Lilly's mysterious plan.

Now she had to prepare for step two.

Heather took another quick look around to confirm no one snuck up on her then cast an invisibility spell before heading for the stairs. Of course the president ended up in the penthouse suite. Only the best the hotel had to offer for someone so important. Ordinarily Heather would've whole-heartedly approved, but tonight she had to walk up ten flights of steps and she didn't appreciate it at all, especially not in four-inch heels.

On the third-floor landing she yielded, kicked the shoes off, and grabbed them before continuing to make her way up.

When she reached the president's floor, she paused and peeked through the door's little window. Two agents stood on guard duty. The burly man on the right wouldn't be a problem, but the slim woman beside him glowed in Heather's magical vision. Of course, there'd be at least one wizard on his security detail. She had no way to tell how strong of an enemy she faced, but if the woman made it this high in the agency, Heather would be foolish to underestimate her.

She pushed the door open a fraction. The male guard looked her way and their gazes locked. Heather activated her new power and crushed his will.

The wizard sensed it at once and whirled toward her companion. "What's wrong?"

He didn't reply.

The wizard looked around until her gaze locked with

Heather's. Unlike the weak-willed man, she didn't succumb at once to the domination spell.

Their minds went to war. The agent gasped, face contorting into a grimace as she fought Heather's control.

But in the end, only one of them had the power of a demon lord backing her. The agent's mind yielded and she groaned as her expression went slack.

Heather clenched her fist and grinned as she stepped through the doorway. As she approached the entrance to the president's suite, the guards moved aside, allowing her to pass without a word.

She stopped and turned to the man. "Open it."

He obliged, his expression slack.

"Good. Now you will both behave normally until I give you another order." The door clicked shut behind her and Heather relaxed a fraction, the worst of the immediate danger behind her.

She tossed her shoes beside the bed then stripped off her dress and added it to the pile before settling onto the mattress. Silk sheets caressed her body as she snuggled in to wait.

Heather dozed as time passed, then she sensed her pawns outside coming alert. A second after that the president's voice reached her through the door. His barely audible words sounded tired. "Goodnight, agents. I'll see you in the morning."

As the door opened, Heather sat up in bed. His eyes widened a fraction before her spell kicked back in and he transformed into her puppet once again.

"You know, you're only the second man to see me naked and look disappointed about it."

Her puppet made no comment as he stood there waiting for an order.

"Right, let's get this over with. Clearly tonight isn't going to be the most passionate night of my life."

She took a moment to set her phone up and point it at the bed. It hung in midair, held in place by a spell. A mental command got the president in place beside the bed and she hit record.

This would be a night he'd never forget, assuming she allowed him to remember what they did.

CHAPTER 19

Conryu paused a couple of feet from the smooth steel wall surrounding the elf ruin. The path they'd been following stopped dead at the base. No gate marred the metal, no runes or ethereal markers indicated the presence of a portal. The path just ended at a blank section of wall. How the hell did they bring the logs inside and who built a wall with no gate?

Maria had warned him elf ruins were dangerous, and the one in Central America proved her right, but he found them more annoying than deadly.

More to assuage his curiosity than because he thought he'd find anything, Conryu made a slow circle around the ruin. On either side of him, the girls kept their heads on swivels. He found that very reassuring. Nothing like three alert ninjas to ensure nothing snuck up on you.

Five minutes of walking brought them back to where they began. As he expected, he found no way in. Conryu glared at the steel, willing a door to appear. It ignored his mental command, mocking him in a way that should have been impossible for inanimate metal.

"Well, if we can't go through, we'll have to go over. Gather around."

The girls pressed close and he summoned a disk of light magic that lifted them up to the battlements. They stepped onto the heavy steel walkway. Every moment he expected some kind of guardian to appear, but so far, they had the place to themselves.

He couldn't make up his mind if that was a good thing or not.

Conryu squinted against the glare of the sun. The courtyard looked like a deserted shipyard. Tools and scraps of wood littered the ground, but the workers remained a mystery. He looked up at the canopy. How could a flying ship pass through there without smashing branches and exposing the clearing for anyone to see? None of it made sense.

Tamaki gestured to a nearby wall tower. "Perhaps we'll find something in there, Chosen."

"Couldn't hurt to take a look." He set out along the battlements. His foot slipped a bit on the walkway. The surface had an unnaturally smooth appearance, almost like someone had polished the metal. Why someone would polish a walkway, he had no idea. Yet another mystery, like everything else in this miserable place.

They reached the tower, which conveniently had a door, and slipped inside. From the outside the walls looked like solid steel, but from the inside he could see right through to the jungle. What a cool trick. No one would be able to tell if or how many guards manned the tower. Only dust and cobwebs decorated the walls and floor. From the looks of it,

Conryu doubted anyone had cleaned the place since the elves fled Earth.

He glanced out at the courtyard, but the new angle revealed nothing useful, just more questions without answers. The most pressing ones being where did whoever built the flying ship come from and where did they go?

He swallowed a sigh. One step at a time. Much as he'd like to wrap this up in a hurry, rushing would only lead to mistakes, and mistakes in this business could be deadly.

"Let's head down and take a closer look at the central tower."

They went back out on the battlements and Conryu used another disk of light magic to lower them to the ground.

As they picked their way through the debris field, he asked, "Can you shift to the borderland?"

Kai shook her head. "No, Chosen. The barrier prevents it."

As expected, but it would've been nice to catch a break. "Then we'll have to be extra careful."

As if the universe heard him, a faint vibration ran through the ground. A moment later an opening formed in the tower's solid steel wall. It looked like the metal liquified and shifted around. He'd never seen anything like it and assumed some sort of earth magic caused the effect. Then again, the elves used magic in a completely different way than the wizards of Earth did. Best not to make assumptions.

Something moved in the darkness and a moment later a monstrous shape emerged. The machine gleamed in the light. Made of the same polished metal as everything else around here, it rolled forward on four giant wheels, two massive tentacles emerging from its sides. One ended in a grasping, claw-like hand that clanked as the fingers opened and closed. The other ended in a spinning circular saw which explained how they harvested the trees.

The girls all had their swords out in an instant, though Conryu doubted they'd do much against the huge construct.

The behemoth accelerated, tentacles flailing.

Everyone scattered.

Tamaki darted in as it passed. Her sword flashed and sparks flew as she sliced across its flank.

The blow hardly left a scratch.

Kai attacked from the other side with equally poor results.

As expected, physical attacks, at least those made with the weapons they had on hand, amounted to nothing.

Conryu leveled the staff and the crystal tip turned black. A stream of dark magic raced out, enveloping the construct. Now connected by magic, he could sense the core powering the machine, buried deep in the center of its huge metal body.

He pushed hard, trying to drive his spell deeper into the metal, but it resisted.

"You have to soak it in dark magic, Master," Prime said.

At the rate the construct was rolling his way, Conryu didn't think he had time. Instead he reshaped the spell into a drill and rusted his way into the construct's body.

The girls did their best to try and distract it, but the construct had clearly dismissed them as no threat. Normally an unwise decision, but in this case Conryu couldn't fault its logic. Black iron made short work of flesh, but against metal they might as well not bother.

He'd rusted three-quarters of the way to its core when the construct finally finished turning. Its wheels crushed scraps of wood as it rushed him.

Conryu threw more power into his spell as sweat poured down his face.

Man, this was going to be close.

At ten yards away, he hit the core and snuffed it out.

Unfortunately, the construct's momentum kept it rolling right at him. Tamaki tackled him from the right and they rolled out of the way together, ending up in a tangled heap, their faces inches apart and Tamaki on top of him.

"Thanks," he said. "You can get off now."

She scrambled to put some distance between them as Conryu fought not to smile. Sometimes he found their reactions too adorable, even under these circumstances.

Conryu got to his feet and focused on the tower. Minutes stretched as the silence grew ever more uncomfortable. When five had passed he said, "Looks like there was only one of them. Thank heaven for small favors. Lucky for us, the door didn't close when we destroyed the construct. Maybe we'll find something more interesting inside."

Conryu strode through the doorway, Kai on one side, Tamaki on the other and Kanna on rear guard. Beyond the entry area, not so much as a spark of light broke the darkness. He summoned a sphere of holy light which revealed a whole lot of nothing, just a dusty passage deeper into the tower. He doubted they'd find more shadow beasts here, but the holy energy made him feel better all the same.

They moved methodically, checking each room they passed for signs of activity and finding nothing beyond dust and stale air. At least until they reached the final room of the ground floor. There they found an alchemy lab virtually identical to the one in the Darien Gap ruin. The only difference between this lab and the other was a spell circle on the floor. He had no idea what it did and made sure to give it a wide berth.

Unlike the rest of the tower, this room had seen recent use. No dust covered the floor and all the equipment appeared perfectly maintained. He had trouble picturing demon cultists using a facility like this. Given all they'd seen, heart hunters struck him as more likely, but as far as he knew, the elf-bloods only lived in Central America. Of course, given what people knew about Africa in this day and age, whole tribes of heart hunters could call the continent home and no one would know.

"What do you think they were making in here?" Kanna asked.

"Hard to say, but amphibious troops seems like a good guess," Conryu said. "Move back, I'm going to put as much of this stuff out of commission as I can."

They cleared the room and he hit it with bursts of dark magic that shattered glass test tubes and warped the metal benches, but didn't touch the cylinders along the wall. Once again the durability of elven craftsmanship shone through.

When he'd done all he could, they resumed the search. Walking through the silent halls, Kai asked, "There are no tracks in the dust, so how did whoever used it reach the lab?"

"Beats me. That's one of many questions I'd like answered."

They continued their search, room by room and level by level. But they found nothing of interest. Looked like the locals had gathered up everything they could and relocated. Perhaps to the temple of Narukami Tempest.

At last, they reached the top floor. The entire space consisted of a single room. Intricate rune circles had been carved into the floor, connected by lines that formed a complex web.

Conryu didn't have a clue about elf magic and he couldn't begin to guess what the circles did. Best not to mess with them until they figured something out.

"Prime, any thoughts?"

"No, Master. My knowledge of elf magic is extremely limited. They had little to do with dark magic after all."

"Right, okay. I'm definitely going to need help with this. Kanna, get outside the barrier and fetch me a squad to watch the tower. They're going to have to be inside the barrier, so no rookies."

"Yes, Chosen.' Kanna bowed and hurried away.

Putting her out of his mind, Conryu took out his phone and took multiple pictures of the circles from every angle. Maria had done a bunch of research on elf ruins, maybe she could make heads or tails of them. No way would he bring her here in person. If she couldn't figure out what they did from the pictures, they'd have to find some other way forward.

Ten minutes later Kanna returned with three other ninjas. Conryu frowned. That was one short of a full squad.

She must've noticed his expression. "This is the rest of my squad, Chosen. If you require an experienced team, there are none more experienced than us."

He hated to risk Kanna, but in this case it might be wise. "Okay, I want you to watch this room. Anything happens, don't try to be heroes, escape and let me know as soon as you can. Okay?"

"As you command, Chosen," Kanna said. All four ninjas bowed as Conryu led Kai and Tamaki out of the room and back outside. Once they were clear of the barrier, he opened a portal and returned to the borderland.

"What now, Chosen?" Kai asked.

"Maria has done some research on elf artifacts. She might be able to figure out these rune circles."

"Master," Prime said. "You do realize it's late at night in Central."

Conryu had not, in fact, realized that. "Okay, plan B. We let Maria sleep and ask Narumi if she knows anything about them."

He concentrated and called out to the former grandmaster. While they waited, Prime said, "Sleeping is what you should be doing, Master. It's been nearly a day since you slept at the Kanes' apartment."

"That's not so bad for me." Before Prime could say anything he continued. "But your point is well taken. Once we talk to Narumi, I'll get some rest."

It didn't take long for Narumi to appear. Most of the black-winged angels didn't have much in the way of day-to-day duties as far as he could tell. Which came in handy for him, but must be boring for them.

"How may I serve, Chosen?" Narumi asked.

Conryu pulled out his phone, opened the first image, and handed it to her. "Do those mean anything to you?"

She studied the picture, a little frown turning her perfect red lips down. "They're elf runes, that much I can say for certain. As for their purpose, I'm afraid I have no idea. Would you like me to research them in the library?"

"That would be fantastic, but I can't give you my phone. How's your memory?"

"Excellent. Give me a few minutes to study them."

"There're half a dozen more if you want to look at them. Just swipe right to left."

The group waited silently as Narumi went from image to image. Eventually she nodded and held his phone out. "I'll do my best to find the information you need quickly, but there are no guarantees."

"Understood, thanks."

She bowed and flew back the way she'd come.

Maybe Prime's suggestion triggered it, but he had to fight a yawn. Time to head back to the real world for a nap.

———

C alint didn't need to sleep the way a human did, but he did find it useful to regularly enter a state of deep meditation to clear his mind and help with focus. So he sat cross-legged on a mat in his private chambers, eyes closed and mind turned inward. His thoughts did not travel a positive path. Everything he'd tried since beginning his mission to conquer the world in his master's name had failed. His servants had proven utterly ineffective against the Reaper's Chosen and Dagon's kraken. At this rate, he would run out of followers before he accomplished anything.

Ending up face to face with an angry demon lord didn't appeal to Calint at all. As an immortal elf-blood he seldom thought about death, but lately it had been on his mind a great deal. The Reaper's Chosen grew closer by the day, he knew it.

As if summoned by his dreary thoughts, a psychic alarm sounded in his mind. Someone had breached the wards of his old fortress. He had a pretty good idea who. Calint had hoped this moment wouldn't arrive for weeks, but as with all his hopes, the universe took great joy in dashing it.

He stood and made his way to the chapel. He'd send Quintus to investigate. Of the remaining hellstorm warlocks, he annoyed Calint the most. If he couldn't win, Calint would at least rid himself of another of the troublesome humans he'd rescued all those years ago.

He found the guardian demon waiting in its usual place behind the altar. It didn't bother acknowledging Calint or opening its eyes. Some of the damage to its outer shell had healed and in his magical vision Calint could see the flow of corruption as the demon absorbed what it needed.

Quintus, to the chapel. I have a mission for you.

The idiot's excitement came through their link. The humans competed constantly for his regard and now that Gaius had fallen, the other three wanted to take his place as what they perceived as Calint's favorite. If only they realized he hated them all equally.

Less than a minute after his summons, Quintus stomped into the chapel. Tall, broad shouldered, and heavily muscled, he stood a head taller than Calint. Once, Quintus had tried to intimidate him. After a day of screaming agony, he realized the error of his ways and didn't try again.

Quintus slapped his gauntlet to his breastplate, making a clatter that set Calint's teeth on edge. He needed quieter servants, no question about it.

"Lord Calint, what are your orders?"

"Someone has breached the ward around my fortress. Gather your troops and travel there via the rune circle. Kill everyone you find and bring their bodies to me." Calint needed every bit of his self-control not to wince when Quintus saluted again. "Good luck."

"Luck?" Quintus said. "Rest assured, my lord, that with my skill in magic and leadership, no luck will be required. I will defeat these intruders without fail."

Calint nodded as if he imagined this fool capable of such a feat. "Excellent, I'm expecting great results. Off you go."

Quintus turned on his heel and marched back out. Either he'd deal with the intruders, or he'd die trying. Or, better yet, he'd kill them and die in the process, ridding Calint of two nuisances at once.

He didn't want to get his hopes too high given the many failures so far on this mission.

CHAPTER 20

Conryu grimaced and blinked a couple of times as he awoke. After parting ways with Narumi, he'd returned to the real world and ducked into his library for a rest. He'd set time to flow at a rate that would have him wake up around seven in the morning Central time. Maria had usually finished getting ready to go to work by then.

He sat up and found Kai still on duty by the door. He'd left it visible in the real world with Tamaki keeping watch from the borderland. If anyone needed him, she'd be able to knock and let them know. Since Kai hadn't shaken him awake, he figured nothing happened during his nap. Still, she could be overprotective and if she decided a particular bit of news didn't add up to an emergency, she might've chosen to let him sleep.

"All quiet?" Conryu asked, his voice still scratchy.

"Yes, Chosen. It has been peaceful since you fell asleep."

Conryu couldn't make up his mind whether that was a

good thing or not, but he did feel much better rested now, so he decided to think of it as a net positive.

"Do you need a nap?" he asked. "I can stop time if you want to rest for a few hours."

Kai shook her head, exactly as he knew she would. "No need, Chosen. We're trained to go for extended periods without sleep."

"Right. Time to go see Maria, assuming I set the flow of time correctly. But first, Galen?" The ghostly librarian appeared and Conryu showed him the pictures he'd taken of the elf runes. "Do these look familiar?"

After a moment of study Galen shook his head. "Alas, no. I apologize for my recent inability to be of help."

Conryu shrugged and pocketed his phone. "Hey, what you don't know, you don't know. It can't be helped."

He was about to shift them to Central when he remembered Tamaki waiting outside. "Kai, you can join Tamaki in the borderland. I'll meet you two at Maria's place."

She bowed and slipped outside.

Now back to business. He visualized the door to the Kane family's apartment. When he opened the library door he found it a stride away. Perfect.

He knocked and soon Mr. Kane, dressed in a black suit with a blue tie, opened the door. "Conryu, good morning. Come in and join us for breakfast."

The savory aroma of sausage drifted out, making Conryu's stomach rumble. "Smells good, thanks."

He followed Mr. Kane to the dining room. Maria looked up from her phone and smiled at him. "Hey, this is a nice surprise. How's everything going?"

"I've hit a bit of a dead end. Do you want to hear about it before or after breakfast?"

"It's going to be another ten minutes!" Mrs. Kane said from the kitchen.

Mr. Kane sat at the head of the table. "I'd like to know what's going on."

Sounded like they had enough time, so he laid out what he'd learned so far. "I'm pretty sure those rune circles are somehow connected to Narukami Tempest's temple, but I have no idea how, what they do, or how to activate them."

"Let me see," Maria said.

He texted her the pictures. "Narumi is researching them in the Reaper's library, but I figure the more people working on this the better."

Maria studied the images, her brow furrowing. After a long moment, she looked up and shook her head. "I've never seen runes like these before, sorry."

"It's fine. I wasn't overly optimistic anyway. Considering where we found them, I doubt any human has ever seen them."

Mrs. Kane came out of the kitchen with four plates floating in the air behind her. She wore a formal white robe today which likely meant she had a consulting job. Maria's mom divided her time between freelance jobs and helping at the Department. Private contracting paid way better and she hated to give up the extra money.

As soon as the plate landed on the table in front of him, Conryu dug into the sausage and eggs. Mrs. Kane knew her business and everything turned out perfectly cooked and delicious. They ate in silence, just enjoying a moment of peace and normalcy.

Conryu finished the last bite of his breakfast and stood. "I appreciate the meal, but I need to resume the hunt. Though what I'm going to do is the real question."

"The Department has a back door into the ruin explorers' database. I'll see if I can find anything as soon as I get to work," Maria said.

He leaned down and kissed her forehead. "Thanks. Anything you can do would be great. Send a ninja for me if you learn anything. I doubt I'll be in cellphone range for a while."

"Try to be careful."

"I'll do my best." Conryu could offer her nothing more and they both knew it. They didn't like it, but they knew it.

———

Kanna stood motionless in the shadows of the steel doorway, her gaze locked on the cavernous chamber beyond. Hours had passed with no movement, no whisper of sound except the rhythmic breathing of her team resting on the landing behind her. They'd been trading off every hour to stay sharp.

Despite the mind-numbing tedium, Kanna's focus never wavered. Endless drills during her early days as a Daughter had honed her patience to near inhuman levels. Despite their talent, she'd feared the younger Daughters might lose their concentration on such a tedious mission. An unworthy thought, but she refused to risk failing the Chosen's mission. Still, she wished whatever he feared might happen would do so sooner rather than later.

Perhaps fate was listening. A faint glow from one of the runes covering the metal floor caught her eye. Soon a second burst to life, then another and another. The pace accelerated until half the runes were glowing.

"Wake up," Kanna said. "Something's happening."

The other Daughters sprang to their feet, all signs of weariness instantly banished by the prospect of danger.

When the final rune blazed to life, humanoid silhouettes took shape within the glow, still indistinct, but growing clearer by the second.

Kanna tensed, pressed herself against the wall, and crouched well below eye level. That should minimize the chances of whatever appeared from the rune circle noticing her. She needed to confirm what had arrived then escape to warn the Chosen.

The glow dimmed, revealing a human figure clad in archaic Roman armor. He had a powerful presence. The air crackled around him with an ominous aura. Crimson eyes smoldered beneath a plumed helmet and an elaborate breastplate covered his chest. Lightning sparked across his skin and armor.

Around him, nightmare creatures took shape, grotesque amalgamations of man and shark, with glowing red eyes and jagged rows of serrated teeth. Similar but less-elaborate armor covered their muscular gray bodies. Webbed hands ending in rending claws flexed as they looked around the room.

Kanna swallowed hard. These monsters matched the description of the ones the Chosen fought earlier. Which meant the armored man had to be another hellstorm warlock. Before she could give the signal to withdraw, the warlock's head snapped around, his gaze locking onto their hiding spot.

No sense bothering with stealth now. "Run!"

They turned as one and sprinted down the steps. Kanna took them three at a time. The sooner they escaped the cursed barrier, the sooner they could shift to the borderland and find the Chosen.

The walls blurred as they raced downward. Part of Kanna hated running from any enemy, but she had her orders and doing anything else while the wards limited their powers would likely end with them dead. Kanna didn't have such a swollen ego that she'd let her people die to soothe it.

Behind them, the crash of stomping feet confirmed the enemy's pursuit. It sounded like they had a decent lead, hopefully enough of one to let them escape. Kanna gritted her teeth. They had to escape. Failure would bring dishonor to the Daughters and she wouldn't stand for it.

They burst into the entrance hall. Kanna's lungs burned and her heart raced. Clearly she needed to spend more time on her cardio training. The Daughters' shifting ability meant they seldom had to run long distances. She made a mental note to add more running to the training schedule.

These thoughts flashed through her mind before she saw the welcoming committee.

Ten of the shark-men stood between them and the exit. How had they gotten down here ahead of them? Nothing had passed them on the stairs and they'd found no other way to traverse the floors when they searched the place earlier. Kanna shook her head. She could puzzle it out later, assuming they survived.

Kanna and her team charged, black iron swords ready. "Break through! Get to the courtyard!"

Despite their limitations, the team fought well. They'd been fighting together for years and each knew what the other would do before they did it. Kanna cut the hand off one of the monsters as it tried to slash her teammate.

The battle soon devolved into a blur of movement. Slash, stab, dodge, and repeat, until the monster in front of her fell.

Strike by strike they inched closer to the exit.

The monsters fought defensively, showing more intelligence than she would've expected from something so ugly.

A bolt of lightning ripped past, close enough to singe her hair.

Kanna whirled.

The warlock had caught up and he'd brought more sharkmen with him.

"Grandmaster!" one of the others shouted.

The team had opened a path and Kanna had no intention of wasting it. "Go! Shift as soon as you're clear."

They sprinted into the courtyard, weaving a random path as lightning bolts exploded around them.

Kanna put on an extra burst of speed and reached the tower door first. She ripped it open and waved the others through.

She followed and slammed it shut behind her an instant before a lightning bolt blew it inward. The heavy blow sent spasms of pain through her back.

Strong hands gripped her arms as the others half carried her up the stairs. Kanna gasped for air and shuffled her feet as the feeling slowly returned to her legs. The explosion left her ears ringing, but even so the pounding footsteps behind them came through clearly. The enemy rushed to catch them and Kanna doubted they'd escape a second battle.

When they reached the battlement, she'd caught her breath enough to shout, "Jump!"

They leapt as far out as they could.

Kanna cleared the barrier only feet from the ground.

She shifted to the borderland. Never had the darkness felt so welcoming.

The team floated, trembling, each trying to catch her breath and recover from the near-death experience.

Much as she would've liked to give them more time, Kanna didn't dare delay. They had to alert the Chosen before the enemy escaped.

CHAPTER 21

Vincent woke to an awful headache. Dim light filtered through the curtains. He rubbed his eyes in a vain attempt to clear the fog from his mind. What had brought on that nightmare last night? He remembered little of it, but his whole body ached from the tension.

He shifted and realized he didn't have any pajamas on. He never slept in the nude. The agents had warned him not to specifically, in case they had to evacuate at night.

Two glasses of Scotch wouldn't be enough to leave him in this kind of state. Should he get up or give himself more time to gather his wits? Neither option thrilled him. What time were they leaving for Central? His addled brain refused to provide the information he needed.

Someone shifted beside him. Panic sent a bolt of adrenaline through him which blasted away his exhaustion at least. Melissa? No, his wife hadn't come on this trip.

Then, who...?

Horror surged through him when a very naked Heather James tossed the covers aside, a knowing smirk twisting her lips. Vincent jerked upright. This couldn't be happening. Maybe he hadn't really woken up yet.

"You're definitely not still asleep," Heather said. "Though I am offended you remember last night as a nightmare. I wasn't that rough with you."

Vincent tried to shout for the agents outside, but the words lodged in his throat. He clawed at his neck. Why couldn't he speak?

"Calm yourself. I've freed your mind enough for us to chat, but nothing more." Heather's mocking tone put a chill in his gut.

Panic bubbled up in the back of his mind, but he forced it down. He couldn't do anything now save keep his wits and think. "What do you want?"

"That's a much better attitude. You're going to help me set a trap for Conryu Koda."

Vincent stared for a moment, certain he must've misheard. He couldn't imagine anyone he'd less want to set a trap for. Had Heather lost her mind? Her actions so far certainly argued that she had. Unfortunately it seemed she retained full control of her faculties, which meant she imagined she had a chance of winning should she succeed in luring him into her trap.

"Do you realize I undergo regular checks for mind control magic? As soon as I return to Central, the agency wizards will find the spell."

Heather's arrogant smile didn't waver. "You won't be under my control when you leave. But if you don't do as I command, well, let's just say the recordings of our little tryst will find their way to the media. What do you suppose that will do for your chances of reelection? Not to mention a long and happy marriage."

Vincent's blood ran cold. He'd be ruined, and even if Melissa understood that he'd acted under the effects of a spell, she'd never look at him the same way. Heather had him cornered, trapped, and he could do nothing about it. Not yet at least.

"What do you want from me?"

Heather rolled out of bed and started getting dressed. "Simple, you'll do whatever I tell you. I've already programmed my number into your phone. When I call, answer, and do what you're told. What could be simpler?"

"And if I do, you'll delete the video?"

"Maybe. At a minimum I won't send it to the tabloids. That's the best offer you're going to get."

He slumped back on the pillows. "Understood. I'll be waiting for your call."

She leaned across the bed and patted his cheek. "That's a good boy. With such an obedient attitude, I'm sure we're going to get along fine."

———

Heather stepped out of the swirling blue portal and stumbled across the Italian marble floor of her stolen penthouse apartment. The usual farewell caress of her aligned element changed into more of a kick in the ass as the gateway slammed shut behind her.

"Damn it." Heather had never felt so unwelcome, so rejected, by the water spirits. It didn't take a genius to figure out why. Her new pact with Ardent Lilly had to be the cause. Did trading away her soul somehow change her from water aligned to dark? She didn't know and had no one she could ask.

Swallowing a sigh, Heather made her way toward the bathroom. The apartment's legitimate owner had already left for work. She allowed him to live his normal life, only seizing control of his mind when he returned. That way he could make more money for her to spend.

Well done, my dear. You did a fine job placing the president under your thumb. I knew I chose well when I made a pact with you.

"Thanks. So what now?"

Now we move to the next phase. Ardent Lilly's hypnotic voice resonated in her head. *In three days, the president is scheduled to attend a soiree at the estate of a wealthy supporter in Central, a man by the name of Durst. You must travel there and set the trap.*

Heather arched an eyebrow. "And the details of this trap? No, let me guess, you'll tell me later?"

I won't just tell you. When the time comes, I will guide your hand myself. Everything must be done perfectly to make the magic powerful enough to defeat such a strong enemy.

The dark weight of the demon lord's presence vanished.

Heather fumed as she peeled off her dress. Ardent Lilly loved doling out morsels of information, keeping her on a need-to-know basis like some expendable underling. Which, much as her ego hated to admit it, described Heather's new position perfectly. Making a deal with a demon might be stupid, but lying to yourself about your place in the partnership doubled the stupidity.

Not that she'd done anything especially clever lately. Curious, she dug out her phone and looked up the Durst family. The first entry indicated they made their money through investing. They owned a number of businesses under the umbrella of Durst Holdings. They had a toe dipped into every pot as it were, though real estate made up the bulk of their holdings.

Her lips quirked up when she found a map of the place. The Durst estate was only a few blocks from the Kincades' mansion. It amused her that her revenge would happen so close to the home of the one who reduced her to her current state. Pity Malice already died. Heather wanted to kill the hag personally.

But life held many disappointments. If anyone could attest to that, Heather could. Well, best get cleaned up and on her way to Central. She had a trap to set.

CHAPTER 22

Quintus couldn't help smiling as the enemy fled before him. Though he would never admit it out loud, he'd been a bit nervous when Lord Calint sent him to slay the intruders who dared enter his fortress without permission. Gaius's death had left all the warlocks on edge. If someone had the strength to kill one of them, then any of them might be in danger.

But these women in black were no match for him and his troops. They ran across the courtyard, somehow dodging his lightning bolts while outpacing his shark-men. He had to give them credit for speed if not courage or strength. They reached a tower just ahead of another spell.

Quintus took some satisfaction from destroying the door, at least until he remembered who owned this fortress. But Lord Calint shouldn't be upset with him for damaging it in the course of completing his mission.

The women raced out of the tower and onto the battlements. Quintus leveled his sword, but before he could loose another lightning bolt, they leapt over the side.

"No!" He called the winds and flew up on the battlements.

Instead of finding bodies crushed at the base of the wall, he found nothing save bare earth. The enemy had escaped.

Quintus snarled. His lord wanted them dead and their bodies returned to him. Letting them escape... No, driving the intruders from the fortress. That sounded much better.

He glided back to the courtyard, sending a psychic command to his troops to assemble as he landed. Soon enough the ugly things stood facing him, their red eyes focused. Though he found them vile, Quintus couldn't deny their superiority to his old legionnaires. Stronger, tougher, and totally obedient, if they'd had troops like this in the empire, Rome would rule the world to this day.

"Spread out and stay alert lest the enemy try to return. I must contact Lord Calint and report our victory."

Why he bothered to spin their failure to the stupid monsters he had no idea. Quintus sat and closed his eyes. His connection to his coreligionists allowed him to speak mind to mind with them, but it required total focus.

You failed, Lord Calint said as soon as he made contact.

"I drove them out of the fortress, my lord. The cowards fled before us and escaped before we could fully engage. I know you hoped for a better result, but the fortress is ours once more. Surely that's the most important thing."

Your stupidity depresses me, Quintus. Those women you let escape are servants of the Reaper's Chosen. Now that they know the fortress is connected to Narukami Tempest, they will return and not alone.

"If the Reaper's Chosen comes here, my lord, I will slay him and bring his head back as a trophy."

See that you do, Quintus. Should you succeed, I will elevate you above the others to serve as my right hand.

Lord Calint's presence vanished and Quintus stood. Slay the Reaper's Chosen. The bold claim had seemed like the right thing to say in the moment, but now that he had a second to reconsider, Quintus didn't know what he'd been thinking. Loath as he was to admit it, Gaius had been both stronger and more skilled than him. If he fell in battle, what hope did Quintus have?

A powerful, dark presence appeared beyond the fortress wall, sending a shiver down his spine. The Reaper's Chosen had arrived. Time for Quintus to live up to his boast.

———

Conryu floated in the borderland, waiting, again, for people to contact him. Kai and Tamaki hovered silently, showing far more patience than he'd ever managed. You'd think, given how much time he spent waiting, he'd have it down cold. Practice was supposed to make perfect after all.

Who would make contact first? They could start a pool, but as far as he knew, the Daughters had nothing to bet with.

He sensed Kanna approaching, which brought a merciful end to his musing. Given their speed, he feared something had gone wrong. Then again, he might be overthinking. Conryu had worrying down to an art form.

When the squad arrived, Kanna tried to bow and made a poor, graceless job of it. She'd never done anything graceless in the time he'd known her. Looked like she'd messed up her back.

"What happened?"

"A warlock showed up." Kanna put a hand on her side. "He hit me in the back with a metal door. Better than getting hit with the lightning bolt the door deflected, but painful all the same. Even worse, he didn't come alone. He brought two dozen of those mutated creatures you mentioned. They looked like a cross between a shark and a man. They came out of the rune circle. We fought our way out, but it was a near thing. Not leaving one of the younger teams was the right decision."

"You did great. Let's head back to the ruin before he escapes." Much as he wanted to heal her immediately, light magic didn't work in Hell.

They flew back the way Kanna had come and emerged a safe distance from the walls of the elf ruin. No monsters manned the battlements. Not that there'd be much point if they had no ranged weapons. Maybe they'd posted lookouts in the towers. He concentrated but sensed nothing through the barrier.

Swallowing a curse, Conryu touched Kanna with the tip of his staff and sent healing energy flowing through her.

She let out a long sigh and said, "My thanks, Chosen."

Now that Kanna had been restored to full strength, they approached the wall. Conryu conjured Cloak of Darkness over each of them. That would offer some protection from the warlock's lightning, though if it was drawn from Narukami Tempest's hell, he feared it wouldn't dispel the magic properly.

"A warlock's connection to his master's hell is far weaker than a true hellpriest," Prime said. "His magical attacks will be equally weakened."

A bit of good news, what a nice change of pace.

They paused at the base of the wall. "Once I lift us up and

over, leave the warlock to me. I want him alive. No need to hold back against the shark things. Everyone ready?"

They all drew their swords and nodded. He lifted the group using a disk of light magic. In the courtyard, a group of shark-men stood in neat rows along with another guy who escaped the set of a Roman epic.

The warlock raised his sword and a lightning bolt shot toward them.

Conryu negated it with a counterburst of dark magic. Then they hit the ground and scattered. The girls raced toward the shark-men while he charged the warlock.

"Reaper's Cloak," Conryu muttered.

The world turned gray when he pulled the cowl into place. A lightning bolt hammered into him, but he felt little more than a tingle, thus confirming Prime's assumption. This guy couldn't hold a candle to a hellpriest.

Conryu could've killed him with a single spell, but he needed this clown alive. Questioning a corpse, while not impossible, didn't work as well as extracting intel from a prisoner.

A second lightning bolt fizzled and then they were face to face.

Conryu swung his staff.

The warlock blocked and counter slashed. The clang of sword on staff mingled with the roars of the shark-men. Vibrations ran through his palms, bringing back memories of sparring in the dojo. The warlock knew his way around a fight but had no hope of winning.

Conryu spun the staff and slammed it into the warlock's side. His breastplate held, but the blow drew a pained grunt.

The warlock said something in what sounded like Latin. He'd never learned the language and had no intention of wasting the tiny bit of power it would take to translate his words.

A sharp thrust hammered into the warlock's chest. At the moment of impact, Conryu released a burst of earth magic, sending the man flying.

The warlock landed hard, the front of his armor caved in.

Not giving him a moment to recover, Conryu charged in and swung again.

The crystal struck the side of the warlock's head and he went limp.

Conryu kicked his sword away then turned to check out the rest of the battle. The girls were holding their own but without their shifting ability couldn't dominate like usual.

He concentrated on the glowing life force in the center of the shark-men's chests. "Null take you all."

Ghostly, skeletal hands shot out from him and snuffed out their life forces. When nothing attacked for a few seconds, he ended Reaper's Cloak and blew out a breath. He'd fought tougher opponents, but this guy still gave him a good workout.

"Everyone okay?"

A few of the girls had shallow wounds that he healed with light magic.

"What now, Chosen?" Kanna asked.

"Now we find out what's really going on here. Someone want to pop his helmet off for me?"

Kai hurried over and removed the warlock's helmet, revealing a surprisingly handsome face. He had an olive complexion typical for someone living in southern Europe, short, dark hair, and a hawkish nose. Only the rapidly forming bruise on the side of his head where Conryu had hit him spoiled his looks.

"Okay my Roman friend, let's see what you've been up to."

He'd done this a few times now and found it easiest to just follow his memories back in time. Conryu charged the tip of his staff with light magic and touched the warlock's forehead.

The view shifted backwards up the stairs to the tower's top floor as if Kanna and her team was chasing them. White light flashed then they stood in a grassy field. The warlock glanced over his shoulder at a dark stone building with jutting towers and a black metal lightning rod on the top. Finally, Narukami Tempest's temple. The portal did lead to it.

Good. Now, how to activate it. He slowed the memories down and focused. The warlock approached a duplicate rune circle on the other side of the portal, took a metal rod out of a hidden sheath in his boot, and touched a specific smaller circle. The runes lit up and they marched through.

So far so good. Now for the temple itself.

He rewound time again and soon found the warlock standing in front of a tall, slim man wearing a dark robe with black eyes shot through with red. Conryu started, so surprised he nearly lost his focus and ruined the spell. The man had long, slightly pointed ears. Not as pointed as Conryu's father, but enough to mark him as an elf of some sort. Maybe a survivor of the war.

If so, he shuddered to think how tough the coming fight might be. Assuming this elf and Morgana had a similar power level, Conryu would have to fight without holding back. Given his magic's damage potential, giving his all might end up rearranging the landscape. Heaven help him if he had to fight in a city.

He released the spell, a faint headache already brewing. A burst of dark magic snuffed out the warlock's life force. Unlike a regular human, Conryu didn't feel bad about finishing him off.

"Chosen?" Kanna asked. "What did you see?"

He rubbed his eyes then ran a hand through his hair. "Trouble. Big trouble. This guy is working for an elf. Gather the rest of the Daughters. If there are more shark-men you're going to have to handle them on your own. I suspect I'll have my hands full."

Since he couldn't keep lifting everyone over the wall, Conryu used earth magic to make a ramp on either side. There, they could come and go as they pleased now.

Kanna hurried away and Conryu turned back to the fallen warlock. It didn't take long to find the foot-long rod of dark metal hidden inside his right boot. Not terribly impressive for the key to the rune circles.

"Come on. Let's find out if this thing works the way it's supposed to." Conryu went into the tower and up the steps to the top chamber. The massive rune circle looked the same as when he left.

He didn't know what the runes meant, but it didn't take long to find the match for the circle he saw in the warlock's memory. If each of the smaller circles led to a different place, it gave their enemy a lot of options for escape. But one thing at a time.

"I'm going to fire it up. Tamaki, take a peek through and see if the temple is visible. Don't go all the way, just a quick check."

He pressed the rune key to the correct circle, and it flared to life. The light spread until they were all lit. "Now."

Tamaki's head vanished then quickly pulled back. "It's there, Chosen. Its corruption is powerful."

Well, he hadn't expected to find a weak temple considering it had probably been there since before the Reaper banished his rivals from this Earth.

Two minutes passed before the rune circle went dark. Now they knew where they had to go and what they had to do. As soon as Kanna arrived with backup, they'd make their final move.

CHAPTER 23

Calint sensed it when Quintus died. Not a surprise given the human's weakness. If he at least managed to do a little damage to their enemy, Calint would consider it a victory.

"Quintus failed," Calint said.

"I'm shocked," the guardian demon said. "I suppose the Reaper's Chosen will be coming here next. He won't get so lucky this time. Together we'll have no trouble defeating him."

Calint shook his head. "No, I have a new plan. I've been thinking about the situation. Even if we win, we won't be able to retrieve the temple core. And the kraken lacks the skills to destroy it. That means it will require the Reaper's Chosen to do it once you've been destroyed. When it turns over the core, I will defeat the human and claim it, then we can start over."

"Your plan requires me to lose this host. I've spent thousands of years strengthening it."

Calint shrugged. "We're stuck without the core. I can think of no other way to claim it. Can you?"

The demon loosed a little growl. "No, but I dislike this all the same. Better to slay the human and come up with a new plan once he's out of the way."

"Do you imagine Dagon will give up the temple core to anyone else? And there's no way we can defeat the kraken in the ocean's depths where Dagon's power is at its strongest. This is the best option. Fight hard, weaken him as much as you can, then die in spectacular fashion. He'll be so relieved to win, nothing else will matter."

"Fine, but if this plan fails, I will ask the master to hand your soul over to me for eternal torment."

Calint shrugged again. "Eternal torment is the reward for failure. Whether you deliver it or some other demon does, my suffering will not change. I will see you when I've reclaimed the temple core."

He left the chapel, warning the remaining hellstorm warlocks as he passed to expect unwelcome visitors. Those two and his troops would no doubt be a total loss. Not a great loss, but an irritation all the same.

Before stepping out of the temple, Calint activated his most powerful stealth spell. It took a lot of power to maintain, but it would ensure he remained hidden from the Reaper's gaze. He would pay any cost to ensure he avoided drawing Null's attention. The demon lord's hatred of his kind knew no bounds.

With his preparations complete, Calint took to the air. He could sense the temple core's location even if he couldn't reach it. He'd find somewhere close to set up his ambush. As his mind raced through possibilities, Calint made peace with the reality that one way or the other, his fate would soon be sealed.

———

I t didn't take Kanna long to return with the rest of the Daughters. When everyone had gathered in the top floor of the tower, he looked them over and took a deep breath. They all stood at attention, their gazes focused on him. Every one of them would die to complete this mission if he gave the order. He saw no sign of fear or hesitation. This responsibility always weighed the heaviest on him. Putting his own life on the line bothered him less than risking others.

He forced himself not to tense up. They had a demon temple to purify and he would see the job done. The consequences of failure didn't bear consideration. He hoped all of them would come back safe and sound, but if the elf survivor came close to matching Morgana's strength or, heaven forbid, he surpassed her, Conryu had no idea how they'd avoid casualties.

Right, time to get this show on the road. "We've finally located Narukami Tempest's temple. I have no idea exactly what forces will oppose us, but I'm confident the battle will be difficult. I'm counting on you all to watch each other's backs. I look forward to celebrating our victory when it's over."

Conryu turned and activated the rune circle. When the final rune lit up, he went through first.

A moment later, he emerged onto an open plain. The Daughters appeared one after the other behind him. The roar of the ocean made it clear they'd moved a long ways from Central Africa. A faint, salty breeze ruffled his hair. A hundred yards away, a dark stone temple loomed against the gray sky. He could sense the corruption from here. Like all the demon lords, it had its own unique flavor of nasty.

Nothing and no one stood between them and the temple. He'd assumed guards would be waiting, but maybe they planned an ambush inside the temple itself.

"What do you make of the barrier, pal?"

"A combination of illusion and a dimensional lock," Prime said. "It reminds me of the barrier surrounding Abaddon's temple. Probably because they were both made by elf magic."

"A dimensional lock means no shifting, right?" Conryu asked.

"Almost certainly, Master. Even without the barrier, this temple is closely associated with Narukami Tempest which means reaching the Reaper's hell would still be impossible."

Prime's analysis matched his expectations, but Conryu hated it all the same. He also couldn't do anything about reality.

"Let's go." He led the way with Kai and Tamaki at his side.

Nothing troubled them as they approached. Conryu, and more importantly Prime, kept his senses peeled, but if any traps protected the place someone had hidden them well. The lack of traps actually made a certain amount of sense if troops came and went from the rune circle on a regular basis. Wouldn't want to blow up your own troops by accident.

Twenty yards from the temple, the front doors opened. A modest horde of shark-men came pouring out to form a menacing wall in front of the entrance. Lightning cracked overhead, the flash reflecting in the monster's dead, black eyes. A pair of hellstorm warlocks stood in front of the group, their armor freshly polished and their swords crackling with lightning.

Conryu leveled his staff and loosed a sphere of dark magic. The warlocks tried to counter it with wind and lightning, but the dark magic negated their spells.

The sphere exploded in the midst of the shark-men, rotting some to nothing and removing bits of others further out.

"Go!" he shouted.

The ninjas charged, watching their spacing so any spells hurled their way would be unable to hit two of them at once. Not that Conryu planned to give the warlocks time to cast.

Ignoring the shark-men, Conryu focused on the spellcasters. He debated using Reaper's Cloak, but the spell took a lot out of him and he still had an elf and a guardian demon to deal with.

He sent lances of white-hot flame rushing out at the two men. They conjured wind barriers which turned the fire aside.

As they exchanged spells, the snarls of shark-men mingled with the clash of blades. He couldn't spare any of his power for the girls at the moment. He needed to deal with these two in a hurry.

He slammed the butt of the staff on the ground, sending a shockwave rushing toward them.

Gusts of wind carried them to safety. Once they were in the air, Conryu had a clear shot at them.

A full-power blast of Divine White Flames rushed out,

smashing easily through the wind barriers they conjured and reducing the pair to ash

With the threat of enemy magic removed, Conryu focused on the melee raging around him. The girls held their own even with their magic limited. Though stronger, the shark-men lacked discipline.

A couple ninjas had been wounded so he healed them with light magic. Conryu focused on healing and conserving his strength. The fight dragged on longer than he would've liked because of that, but he also kept any of the Daughters from getting killed.

A more than acceptable trade as far as he was concerned.

When the battle ended, Conryu focused on the temple. They'd won the easy battle. Things would only grow harder from here. "Kanna, take the Daughters and secure the perimeter. It's too tight inside for all of you to join me. Kai, Tamaki, it'll be the three of us as usual."

Kanna didn't argue, but from the crinkling around her eyes he could tell she wanted to. Instead, she signaled the Daughters and got them into position.

With his exit secure, Conryu took a steadying breath and marched forward, into the temple. Five feet into the entry hall, an eerie bluish glow filled the passage. The light came from floating spheres of crackling electricity hovering near the high, vaulted ceiling. The orbs cast strange, shifting shadows across the black stone walls. The faint smell of ozone mingled with corruption in the air. He approached the first orb, dark magic at the ready, but the spheres didn't react at all. Looked like they just served as a creepy light source.

Alcoves set at regular intervals along both sides of the hall each held a stone statue of a handsome man dressed in dark armor and holding a lightning bolt. Seemed a bit too good looking for a demon lord. Maybe the carvers feared to make an accurate depiction.

Halfway down the passage it split off to the left and right. Conryu paused, but sensed nothing in either direction. The guardian demon's overwhelming aura of corruption came from dead ahead.

"Sense anything, Prime?"

"Nothing in particular, Master. I doubt there's anything living left in this place."

That matched Conryu's feeling. "Straight ahead it is then."

They continued deeper into the temple. Every second he expected something to attack them and every second nothing did. The hall ended in an enormous chapel. A massive, vaulted ceiling arched high overhead, supported by thick stone columns carved with swirling storm patterns. Blue-white lightning orbs floated near the top, bathing the chamber in an eerie electric glow. At the far end, a huge statue of Narukami Tempest loomed, its cruel, handsome face illuminated by crackling energy.

The hideous monstrosity waiting in front of the altar drew Conryu's gaze. The guardian demon, a hulking insectoid abomination covered in segmented black plates like a grotesque beetle, glared at them with blood-red eyes. Lightning arced and danced across its carapace with a constant electric sizzle. It looked recovered from their first encounter.

When it didn't immediately attack, Conryu asked, "Where's the elf?"

"Fled, the miserable coward." The demon's deep voice crackled like a staticky speaker.

"I can't imagine that will go over well with your master." As they talked, Conryu cast subtle spells to protect Kai and Tamaki from lightning and corruption.

"The elf will get what he has coming when the master collects his soul. You would do well to worry about yourself."

The demon roared and hurled a lightning bolt at Conryu, who negated it with a ball of dark magic. Seeing its magic fail enraged the demon. It spread its claws wide and launched itself at Conryu.

A blast of divine white fire hit the demon square in the face. Its roar of rage turned to one of pain as it broke off and soared up toward the ceiling. Conryu hated fighting flyers, especially in an open place like this where they had room to maneuver.

The demon rained lightning bolts down on them as gusts of wind threatened to knock Conryu off his feet. It was like fighting in a hurricane.

A bubble of dark magic formed around Conryu and his companions, ending the barrage and the wind. Kai and Tamaki looked at him, but Conryu had no orders to give. Flinging random spells would only tire him out. He needed a way to lock the demon down, even if only for a second.

He snapped his fingers when the answer came to him. "Get ready. Try to stab it through the gaps in its armor. I've already warded you both against lightning and corruption, so you don't need to worry about that. That thing's claws, on the other hand, should worry you a great deal."

The dark dome vanished and he thrust his staff toward the demon. Chains of pure light magic shot out, wrapping around the demon and dragging it down to the floor.

It roared and thrashed, shattering chains almost as fast as Conryu could conjure them.

Kai and Tamaki approached from opposite sides. As soon as it spotted them sneaking closer, the demon calmed and watched with narrow, glowing eyes. Its position left them with no openings, but now that it had stopped thrashing about Conryu could attack himself.

He sent divine white lightning crackling down the chains. The demon laughed for the instant it took the holy energy to strike it. Though the spell took the form of standard lightning, it used only light magic without a bit of electricity mixed in. The demon's resistance didn't help in the least and it howled as the holy energy burned away its corrupt essence.

With a mighty flex of its wings and arms, the demon shattered his chains and scattered the magic into motes of light. Taking advantage of the opening its movement provided, Kai and Tamaki charged in.

Tamaki drove her sword through its back with enough force to burst the tip of her sword out its chest. Kai hit a moment later, finding a gap in its left thigh armor and slicing halfway through its leg.

The demon howled again.

Quick slashes of its claws forced the girls to leap away before they could strike again. Even worse, Tamaki's sword remained stuck in the monster's chest.

As it gathered itself to leap skyward, Conryu conjured hands of earth magic that grabbed it by both ankles, keeping it from escaping. He drew a circle in the air over the demon's head and called down a pillar of holy energy.

The light burned so bright he could only see the demon as an outline. Black smoke filled the air as the magic burned the demon away.

After ten seconds he ended it. The pillar reduced the demon to a ruined, steaming husk. Kai took a step, but he caught her arm. If it hadn't vanished, some demonic essence must've survived.

Conryu leveled the staff again and sent out a stream of Divine White Flames. He didn't stop until nothing remained but the melted slag of Tamaki's sword.

With the demon gone, some of the oppressive feeling faded away. Now he just needed to purify the place and deal with the temple core.

"Did that seem a bit too easy?" Tamaki asked.

Conryu frowned. "It seemed just as strong as the other guardian demons. Well, not the Horned One's, that golden bull guy was stronger than normal, but it was on par for the rest. It was a guardian demon, right, Prime?"

"Yes, Master. I sensed its essence fleeing back to the temple core when you destroyed its body. It should be there now."

"Good. I'm going to purify the temple first, then we can go deal with the core. Tamaki, you can let Kanna know we're done for now and she and the others can head home. You're welcome to hang out with us or go back to the monastery. The fighting, for the moment at least, is done."

Tamaki bowed and hurried out of the temple.

"What about the elf?" Kai asked.

"I don't know. I'm not too thrilled to know one is still running around after all this time, but I have no idea where to begin looking for him. At least once we destroy the temple core the elf won't be able to turn into a hellpriest."

"An elf can't become a hellpriest in any case," Prime said. "The blood of Heaven prevents it. Most likely this elf has already been transformed into a dark elf."

Since he was in no rush to get started after the fight, Conryu asked, "What's a dark elf?"

"Basically"—Prime went into teacher mode—"it's when an elf's soul is corrupted and bound to a demon lord

Contrary to popular belief, you don't lose your soul once you trade it to a demon lord. Instead, a link is created so that when you die, your soul is dragged to the hell of the lord you serve."

"Huh, I didn't know that. Makes sense though. Alright, let's finish up with this dump and get out of here."

CHAPTER 24

Heather stumbled out of a water portal in the wealthy district of Central. It had taken all her will to force herself through the opening and when she reached her destination, the spirits couldn't kick her out fast enough. At this rate, soon the realm of water would banish her altogether. That would be tremendously inconvenient since she couldn't access Ardent Lilly's hell to serve as a replacement.

Straightening, Heather smoothed her black dress. The Durst estate waited only a block ahead. She'd appeared a safe distance away on the off chance they had a wizard on duty. She cast an invisibility spell and set off for the mansion.

A tall iron fence surrounded the grounds. Hundreds of lights lit it up, turning night into midday. Armed guards patrolled the area in pairs and somewhere a dog snarled. Unlike Kincade Manor, this place had nothing in the way of magical wards. Did the fools really think a few thugs with guns would suffice to protect them?

A few minutes of studying the patrols confirmed a lack of

wizards. Maybe they really did think guns would be enough. She gathered a bit of ether in her legs and sprang over the fence, landing with barely a whisper on the other side.

Two beefy security guards flanked the front doors, assault rifles slung over their shoulders. Invisible or not, only a blind man would fail to notice the door opening. Best to find another way in.

She veered around to the side of the mansion. A servants' entrance waited, unguarded, for her arrival. She tried the handle and found it locked. As if that would be enough to stop her.

Heather pressed a palm to the door, sending a pulse of energy into the mechanism. It clicked open and she slid inside, listening hard for any sign that the guards had detected her arrival. The lavish kitchen she'd entered remained as quiet as a tomb.

Heather sensed fourteen life forces inside the house, most in the main building plus a handful in the east wing. But no one in the west wing. Good, she could use that. Heather liked luxury as much as the next former supermodel, but she never understood why anyone wanted a place with so many unused rooms. A nice penthouse apartment suited her much better.

Plush carpet muffled Heather's steps as she navigated the corridors leading to the west wing. Despite her invisibility, she had the overwhelming feeling that someone would notice her at any moment. Why the idea filled her with such foreboding Heather had no idea.

Her concerns proved unfounded and soon she stood in the doorway of an unused bedroom. Spacious and sparsely furnished, a thin layer of dust made it clear no one had visited the room in some time. A large four-poster bed dominated the center, flanked by ornate nightstands. Heavy drapes covered the windows and an attached private bathroom completed the space. This should suit her needs perfectly.

As soon as she locked the door, Ardent Lilly's voice appeared in her head. *Well done. You won't even have to leave the room.*

Heather forced herself not to grimace at the cold presence slithering around in her head. "What do I need to do now?"

Just relax and open yourself fully to me.

Heather shuddered as Ardent Lilly's presence seeped deeper into her than ever before. Her limbs began to move of their own accord. It felt beyond strange and unsettling to be a passenger in her own body.

Her hands rose, fingers splayed as they traced intricate, unfamiliar patterns in the air. Infernal chants she didn't understand spilled from her lips. The walls and floor pulsed with unholy crimson light as dark magic soaked into them.

The air crackled with gathered energy, raising the fine hairs on Heather's arms as the enchantments took hold. Exactly what they would do, she had no idea, but she knew it would be impressive.

She lost all track of time as Ardent Lilly cast through her body. Eventually, the door rattled in its frame, jolting her out of her trance.

Who could that be? As far as she could tell, no one had used this room in months.

Deal with him, quickly.

Heather regained control of her body just as a man dressed in a black servant's uniform stepped into the room.

He didn't have a chance to speak before their gazes locked and she seized control of his mind.

He stared at her with a slack expression.

"What brought you to this part of the mansion?" she asked.

"I don't know," he said in a dull monotone. "Something felt wrong, so I came to check and make sure all was well."

If an ordinary man could sense their magic, the wizards serving in the president's security detail would pick up on it the moment they arrived.

Don't be concerned. Once the enchantment is laid, concealing magic will ensure no one notices until it's too late. We only need a day to lay the groundwork.

"Bring me something to eat and drink," she said. "And tell the other servants they are not to come this way. We're working on important security precautions for the president's visit. Understand?"

"Yes, I'll make sure no one else troubles you." He turned and marched back out of the room.

When he'd gone, Heather sagged on the bed, the silk sheets cool against her flushed skin. The exertion of channeling Ardent Lilly's magic left her more exhausted than any magic she'd ever done.

"How much longer is this going to take?"

We will continue to strengthen the spells until the day of the event. That will give us the best chance of success.

Heather grimaced but hadn't expected any other answer. Maybe some food would restore her strength. If it didn't, she had no idea how she'd last two more days.

CHAPTER 25

Conryu stepped out of the now-purified temple, Kai close behind him. He drew in a deep breath of fresh, corruption-free, ocean air. He never figured on having to spend two days purifying the temple, but the corruption resisted with greater tenacity than he expected, a testament to the temple's power. Only the Horned One's temple had caused him more trouble. He'd also taken his time rather than working to exhaustion. The elf's survival kept him from pushing too hard lest he show up at a vulnerable moment.

He glanced up at the clear, blue sky. No trace of the hellish storm remained, which confirmed his success. Now he just had to destroy the temple core to sever Narukami Tempest's link to Earth.

Actually, he had two more things to do. Before dealing with the temple core, he wanted to make sure no one could use this temple again.

Conryu leveled the staff at the cliff below the temple's foundation. The crystal turned brown a moment before he lashed out with a blast of earth magic. The ground trembled and jagged cracks ran through the rock. A deep rumbling grew louder by the second.

The temple shuddered, then, with a thunderous roar, the cliff crumbled. The temple along with tons of rock tumbled into the ocean. He offered a faint smile as the spell ended and the dust settled. Maybe he could call that an offering to Dagon.

"There, you can't get much more thorough than that. Let's go. I'm sure Dagon is eager to hand off the core."

He opened a hell portal and he, Kai, and Prime strode into the borderland. Cerberus lifted his three heads and barked a greeting as his tail wagged. He hadn't expected to find Tamaki standing beside the demon dog.

"You didn't want to go home?" Conryu asked.

"There were no pressing matters requiring my presence at the monastery," Tamaki said. "And I wished to see this mission through to its conclusion."

"That's fine. I don't expect any trouble until I track down the elf, but you're always welcome to hang out with us."

As he prepared to shift them all to the Challenger Deep, a familiar presence approached from deeper in Hell. Narumi's lovely form became clear a moment later.

When she'd stopped and bowed, he asked, "Did you discover something about those rune circles?"

"Yes, Chosen. The smaller circles are each linked to different locations and, depending on which one you activate, it will connect the main circle to a specific place."

"So it's like a transportation network the elves set up?"

"Essentially," Narumi said. "The runes are not inherently dangerous. But figuring out where each one leads would require significantly more research. Of course, you could always activate them one at a time and see where you end up, but that has considerable risks."

"Yeah, I have no interest in ending up at the bottom of a volcano or something. Don't worry about it. The temple's gone and as long as the rune circles aren't dangerous, I don't care about them. Some other researcher can look into them if they want to." That would most likely be Maria given her sometimes obsessive nature.

"As you wish, Chosen." Narumi bowed again. "If there is nothing else, I'll return to Black City."

Conryu nodded. "Thanks again for your help."

Narumi diminished then vanished altogether into the darkness. With the rune circle business on the back burner, he turned his focus back to the temple core. An effort of will shifted them to the Challenger Deep. An almost imperceptible ripple ran through the essence of Hell then he opened a viewing portal. Conryu flinched when the kraken's huge eye filled it. Looked like they'd arrived in the correct place.

You have fulfilled your end of our bargain. Vicious glee filled Dagon's mental voice. *Narukami Tempest has been reduced to nearly nothing on this world.*

"Yup. The elf still has me worried, but I'll deal with him when I find him. So, the temple core?"

My pet shall deliver it to you on the surface. As soon as I sense its destruction, I'll put the kraken back into hibernation.

Conryu blew out a breath and shifted them to the surface. Sounded like Dagon and the Reaper had come to an understanding on something other than hating each other. How novel, not that he planned to complain.

He stepped out of the portal and a flying spell caught him a few feet above the waves. Half a minute later, a monstrous tentacle burst from the depths, its slick, mottled flesh glistening. A gem the size of Conryu's fist nestled in one giant sucker. It pulsed with an eerie blue light the same shade as the globes which lit the temple. Jagged forks of lightning crackled across its surface. This thing certainly gave off the right vibe.

Conryu coated his hand in Cloak of Darkness then took the temple core. Even with his protection in place, the corruption made his hand ache. He had no doubt destroying the core would give him every bit as much trouble as the temple itself.

The kraken's tentacle vanished back under the waves and he wished him a peaceful five-thousand-year nap. Now to find somewhere to land so he could burn away the core. He scanned the horizon with his vision enhanced and soon spotted a small, rocky island jutting from the sea. Conryu flew toward it, eager to finish his mission.

"Master."

Conryu sensed it too, a powerful magical presence, corrupt, but also different from the hellstorm warlocks. He had a bad feeling, but couldn't stop, not now when total victory lay within reach.

A figure in dark robes stood on the sandy beach. His familiar face thin to the point of gauntness and his eyes glowing red, he matched the memory Conryu had seen in the hellstorm warlock's mind. Slightly pointed ears confirmed his identity. The elf, it seemed, had found him. And he didn't come alone. He held a dagger to a young woman's throat. Her wide, terror-filled eyes stared at Conryu, begging for help.

"I knew Dagon would hand the core over to you once you defeated the guardian demon," the elf said, his voice cold and emotionless. "I'll trade you this girl for it."

Conryu's mind raced. He couldn't just hand it over. If he did, many more people would die, sacrificed to rebuild Narukami Tempest's connection to Earth. On the other hand, he couldn't let an innocent girl die. What should he do? His mind raced but no options presented themselves. Against a regular opponent, a simple spell would destroy the dagger, but an elf wouldn't miss the activation.

"Stop wasting my time," the elf said. "I know you heroic types. You won't let an innocent die even when it's the right thing to do. Just give me the core and let's get this over with."

Conryu's jaw clenched. He seldom hated someone at their first meeting, but he happily made an exception in this guy's case. Maybe he could buy some time.

"If you kill her, don't think I'm going to let you walk away. You'll be visiting Narukami Tempest in short order."

"This is my last chance," the elf said. "You've thwarted my every effort and come close to severing my master's connection to this world. If I let you destroy the core without making every effort to stop you, my soul's fate doesn't bear contemplation. Now, her life or the core. You have five seconds to decide."

A dark blur appeared behind the elf and then Tamaki ran her sword through the hostage's back, killing her instantly.

Rage at the utter pointlessness of it exploded through Conryu.

He roared and thrust out his staff, unleashing a torrent of dark magic.

The elf was blasted backward, slamming into a palm tree with bone-breaking force.

Conryu advanced, each step deliberate, measured. Dark power crackled around him, a maelstrom of barely contained fury. Part of his mind had shut down. The part that never wanted to go overboard lest he do something he might regret.

The elf struggled to rise, but Conryu didn't give him a chance.

Blast after blast reduced the elf to a dark stain on the shore. Rocks blackened and the few palm trees withered to nothing. When he came back to himself, everything on the island was dead.

Conryu stood amidst the carnage, chest heaving, the temple core still clutched in his white-knuckled grip. He'd won the battle, if you wanted to call it that. Certainly the dead hostage would no doubt argue about him claiming victory. His lack of restraint scared him more. It reminded him of his battle with Morgana, only he couldn't blame the Reaper this time. He'd hit the elf with everything he had and was reminded once again of both his power and his responsibility to handle it properly.

Safe to say he failed this test in every way possible.

Tamaki appeared before him, knelt, and placed her sword at the edge of her throat. "Forgive me, Chosen. I knew you were too kind to do what had to be done, so I did it for you. I offer my life as payment for my arrogance."

Conryu closed his eyes. Tamaki did what she thought she had to. What he couldn't bring himself to do despite knowing what had to happen. Could he fault her for that? Could he fault her for covering for his weakness?

No, but that didn't make accepting what she did easy. When he had himself fully under control, he took a knee and gently moved her sword away from her skin. "It's alright. I should've been strong enough to keep you from having to do what you did."

She looked up at him. Were those unshed tears in her eyes? Surely not. "Thank you for understanding, Chosen."

He pulled her to her feet. "Return to the monastery. Once I finish destroying the temple core, I'm planning a nice long nap."

Tamaki bowed and shifted to the borderland.

Now to finish this. He turned his attention to the temple core. Conryu tossed the surprisingly pretty crystal on the sand, summoned Divine White Flames, and merged his mind with them.

The demon screamed and begged and wheedled, but he had no mercy for the creature. It bore at least part of the responsibility for what happened here and he had no one else he could punish.

When nothing of the core remained, he sighed, exhaustion rushing over him like a wave trying to drag him under. He stumbled, his knees threatening to buckle.

Kai appeared beside him and took his arm. "I have you, Chosen."

"I know, thanks." He summoned the library. Before he could open the door, his phone rang. How the hell did he have service out here? He checked the number. What did the president want now? Much as he wanted to ignore it, he forced himself to hit connect. "Yes, sir?"

"Conryu, there's going to be a party tonight and a number of important people are eager to meet you. Can you join me?"

He closed his eyes for a moment. Going to some party with a bunch of politicians appealed to him only a fraction more than a rematch with the guardian demon. "Sorry, sir. I'm in the middle of something. Maybe another time."

"It's important." He sounded more desperate than

commanding. Conryu didn't think he'd ever heard the president use that tone. "I'll explain when you arrive, but it's vital that you come."

Conryu swallowed a groan. "What time?"

"Eight o'clock at the Durst estate in Central. It's three doors down from Kincade Manor."

"Fine, but I'm not dressing up."

CHAPTER 26

Conryu emerged from his library a block from the Durst estate with ten minutes to spare. True night hadn't fallen yet, but twilight had about run its course. Twelve hours' sleep and a visit to Giovanni's for pizza did wonders to heal his psyche. He still felt a bit twisted up after what happened with the elf, but he had himself sorted out enough to think straight. Meeting with the great and powerful didn't sit very high on his to-do list. He'd make the rounds then split.

"This is a waste of time," Prime said.

"You're not wrong, pal, but putting in an appearance might save me some trouble down the road. The president sounded pretty on edge and I'm curious why. Somehow, I doubt it's just campaign stress."

Prime turned invisible and Conryu started walking down the sidewalk. He had no trouble spotting the Durst estate. Floodlights lit the place up like a carnival. Shafts of light shone into the air while glowing drift lights floated around the grounds.

Agents from the president's security detail manned a gate in the iron fence. They eyed Conryu as he approached, but by this point pretty much everyone knew him. He also assumed their boss had informed them he'd received an official invitation.

"Evening, fellas," Conryu said. "I think I'm on the guest list."

"Mr. Koda," one of the guys said, his jaw tight and his frown deep. "We were told to expect you. Please don't do anything crazy this time."

Conryu grinned. "Were you on duty when I visited the presidential mansion last time?"

The agent winced, all but confirming his theory. "Yes. No one likes being shown how powerless they are."

"Sorry about that. I was in a bad mood. If it helps, I feel equally powerless every time I visit the Reaper, so I can totally sympathize."

"It doesn't. Go on in. He's mingling, but if you look for the biggest crowd, that'll be the president."

"Thanks." He offered a little wave and strode between the two agents and onto the grounds.

As he walked down a gravel path between shrubs he sensed other agents on patrol. He counted a dozen or so of them scattered around in pairs. Conryu assumed they had some snipers on duty somewhere, but he didn't bother trying to pin them down.

He reached the front door without issue and another pair of agents opened it before waving him in without comment. They kept their expressions completely blank, like they were wearing masks. Did they learn that expression in agent school?

Shaking his head at the pointless thought, he entered and

made his way into a huge ballroom filled with people dressed in tuxedos and gowns. Just the jewelry he saw at a glance would pay off a small country's national debt.

These people should thank their lucky stars he wasn't a thief.

"Conryu?" He grinned as Kelsie, wearing a deep-blue dress and a string of black pearls, hurried his way. The way she wobbled, he feared she might fall off her three-inch heels.

"Hey. I didn't think I'd find you here."

"Since I live just up the road it would've been rude for the Dursts not to invite me. Forget about that, what are you doing here and what are you wearing?"

"I don't know why I'm here, but the president asked me to stop by, so I figured I'd oblige. I told him I wasn't dressing up and I meant it. So how are things going with your new consultant?"

Kelsie offered a big smile. "Mr. Colt has so many interesting ideas. It feels like our magical engineers have moved into my office. Would it hurt anything if I moved the portal?"

"I can't imagine why it would. I moved it halfway across the city without issue."

"Great, there's an empty bedroom I'm thinking of turning into a consultation room so the engineers can work in peace."

"What about you working in peace?"

"That too." Kelsie stood up on her tiptoes. "There's President Langston. You should go say hi. It's poor manners to speak with me before paying your respects."

Conryu snorted. "I'd rather talk to you any day. Still, best find out what he wants. Talk some more later?"

"Sure! We've got a lot of exciting projects in the works."

Conryu loved seeing her in such a good mood. "Cool. I can tell you about my conversation with a kraken. Later."

Kelsie stared at him, mouth partway open, as he walked away. He loved surprising people. Given the many horrible situations he found himself in, he had to find his amusement where he could. Conryu found his mood vastly improved, though how long that would last once he found out what the president wanted remained an open question.

As he got closer to the knot of people surrounding the president, one of the agents nearby spotted him and whispered to his charge. The president spun his way and excused himself from the group.

They shook hands and Conryu asked, "So why am I here?"

"What I have to tell you is best not spoken about with so many people around. Come with me."

The president took him by the elbow and guided him toward a doorway leading into the mansion's west wing. When a group of agents tried to join them, he waved them away. To Conryu's considerable surprise the agents backed off. He figured they went everywhere together.

"Is it okay for you to leave your security behind?"

The president laughed. "Ordinarily, no, but we have a standing protocol that if I'm with you, it's fine. Much as they dislike it, we all know that, should you wish me harm, all the agents on my team wouldn't be able to stop you. And some of the matters we have to discuss are best not overheard by anyone."

Conryu couldn't argue with his reasoning. They passed closed door after closed door as they moved deeper into the west wing. He hadn't seen a single soul, nor did he sense anyone. How far did Langston plan to take him?

He opened the door to the final room in the hall and motioned Conryu through.

Something's wrong, Master. I don't know what, but something has been disguised.

Conryu didn't like the sound of that, but he'd come this far, he could go a little further. As soon as they entered the empty room, Langston said, "I brought him."

The air shimmered and the door slammed shut behind them. Conryu summoned the Staff of All Elements to his hand quick as a blink. The shimmering resolved itself into the familiar figure of Heather James, but she seemed off.

Her soul has been corrupted by a demon contract.

That definitely counted as being off. "What's this crazy bitch doing here?"

"Blackmailing me," the president said. "Bringing you here was the price for her not releasing a very incriminating video. I apologize for the deception."

As apologies went that one was pretty bland, but whatever. "So what do you want?"

"Revenge," Heather said. "Thanks to you my life was ruined. Malice is already dead and I can't get to your girlfriend while you're still alive. So that means you have to die."

Conryu stared at her in utter disbelief. "Revenge? Are you joking? You tried to seduce me so you could collect my genetic material for Malice. All I did was refuse. Then you tried to kill Maria and still I spared you. Despite all that you think I'm in the wrong?"

"I lost everything when I failed Malice. And you're the reason I failed." Darkness leaked out of her body and the room started to vibrate.

The corruption made him sick to his stomach. Conryu

conjured a light magic barrier around himself and the president, cutting off the sick feeling.

"You're not strong enough to kill me," Conryu said. "You traded your soul for nothing."

A new voice, richer and deeper, that oozed darkness spoke through Heather's lips. "Even if you don't die, when the dark bomb we've built consumes my pawn and explodes, hundreds of important people will die. The chaos will be glorious as will Null's irritation."

"He's supposed to die, not me!" Heather said.

"Don't worry," the new voice said. "You will be reborn as a succubus in my hell."

From the almost comically surprised look on her face, no one had mentioned this part of the plan to Heather. Not that it mattered. Conryu couldn't let the bomb explode.

"How do I stop it?" he asked Prime in a low whisper.

You need to burn away the corruption. The spell is keyed to her life force. Once that is consumed, the corruption will explode outward and kill everyone in the mansion and on the grounds.

Great. The way Heather's face twisted in pain, he didn't have long to work.

He leveled the staff and Divine White Flames poured out. Just like when he cleansed a demon temple, Conryu scrubbed away the corruption everywhere he found it. It didn't resist anywhere close to as much as a temple did and he soon had half the corruption dealt with.

She's nearly gone, Master.

Shit! He wasn't going to finish the job in time.

Wait, if the spell was tied to Heather's life, as long as she didn't die, it wouldn't explode. He shifted his beam of light magic to healing and aimed it at Heather. Keeping the bitch alive didn't overly please him but given the alternative he'd deal.

"Kai! Get everyone out of the mansion. Tell them to move as far away as they can. Kelsie can help you."

Now he had to hope they could evacuate before he ran out of strength.

"What about us?" the president asked.

"You got me into this mess, so you're sticking around until the end. Prime, can I move her away from this room?"

"No, Master." Prime had given up on staying invisible and now floated in full view beside him. "Based on the spell's structure that would be the same as if she died, though it would weaken the spell considerably, likely limiting it to destroying the mansion but sparing the grounds."

Conryu could work with that. He raised a hand and blew away the ceiling and roof, exposing the night sky.

Heather had doubled over despite the healing and was clutching herself. Much as he despised the woman, her pain caused him no pleasure. If she'd only had a more modest ego, she could've lived a happy life. Maybe. Okay, maybe not.

Sweat poured down his face and the first tingle of backlash had formed in the back of his mind when Kai whispered in his ear. "Everyone is clear, Chosen."

"Good work, Kai. Stay in the borderland. I'll join you in a sec." Now the tricky bit. "I'm going to cast a spell on you," he said to the president. "Don't be alarmed."

"What—"

Conryu didn't give him time to ask his question before covering him in Cloak of Darkness. Next he pulled Heather closer and opened a hell portal directly under them. He vaguely sensed the explosion as they dropped through.

Kelsie drifted through the gathering, chatting without really registering what anyone said. She couldn't help wondering what the president wanted with Conryu. Nothing good she felt certain. People seldom wanted him for anything good. Maybe she was wrong. Kelsie wanted to think so, but in her heart, she didn't believe it for a second.

She took half a step toward a nearby table to collect a snack, then something tickled her magical senses. It came from the west wing where Conryu went. A moment later a wave of dark magic staggered her.

What in the world?

She wasn't the only one who noticed. The lone woman on the president's security detail, a wizard she assumed, frantically shouted something into the microphone in her cufflink. A murmur ran through the rest of the partygoers as they realized something was wrong, even if they lacked the magical ability to tell what.

Kelsie didn't know what to do. Before she could decide, a ninja appeared right beside her. She about jumped out of her shoes.

"The Chosen says everyone needs to put as much distance between themselves and the mansion as possible. He said you could help me convince them."

"Kai?" The ninja nodded. "I'm not sure what I can do, but I'll try. Do you know what's happening?"

"Someone set a magical bomb and it's getting ready to explode. He's doing what he can to delay the explosion, but it is only a matter of time."

Right, that had to be what the president wanted him for.

"Come on, we'll talk to the agent in charge. I met him when I arrived."

"There's no time. We need to hurry."

"Okay, um, I guess we could just say there's a bomb. That usually gets people moving." She cast a simple voice enhancing spell and shouted. "There's a bomb! Everyone out if you want to live! Don't stop until you're across the street!"

Kelsie could've done without the panic, but everyone did start streaming toward the exit. The nearest agent pushed his way through the crowd to her. "What's this about a bomb?"

Kai explained and said, "The Chosen will protect the president. If you don't wish to die, get your team out."

"We can't leave until we know the president is safe."

"If you wish to die doing you duty, that is your choice." She bowed. "I honor your dedication."

From the look on his face, the agent had already begun rethinking his decision. "Mr. Koda will keep him safe?"

"You may depend upon it," Kai said.

The agent lifted his arm and said, "We're pulling out. Now."

"Go, Kelsie," Kai said. "I will make one last sweep and let him know it's clear."

Kelsie didn't argue. She gave Kai a quick hug and hurried toward the exit as fast as she could manage in her heels. She just made it across the street when Thomas Durst found her and asked, "What in the world is this business about a bomb in my house?"

Kelsie took a breath to explain. Before she could speak a pillar of darkness exploded outward, consuming the entire mansion. She sighed. Whenever Conryu showed up at a party, you knew it was going to be exciting.

CHAPTER 27

Heather screamed when the stream of healing magic ended. Ardent Lilly's presence vanished from her mind, which she appreciated. Sadly, the pain of her magic didn't disappear along with it. For some inexplicable reason the demon lord's betrayal surprised her. Using her as the detonator for a bomb was exactly the sort of thing you'd expect a demon to do. If she had somehow succeeded in killing Conryu, it would've technically lived up to the wording of the contract.

Speaking of, he was floating nearby, beside her own pawn, a look of disgust on his face as he watched her. She clenched her jaw against the pain, unwilling to give him the satisfaction of seeing her suffer.

"Is this Hell?" the president asked.

"Yup," Conryu said. "Now she can explode and not hurt anyone. This whole place is filled with dark magic."

The indifference in his voice when he said she could explode stung, not that she expected anything better.

A sense of dislocation hit her and the next thing she knew

they were standing in a huge throne room surrounded by beautiful women with the wings of ravens and dressed like ninjas. Directly ahead, the Reaper sat on a throne of bones, his cowl focused directly on her. Heather swallowed hard and only the pain kept her from fainting. The president, on the other hand, collapsed on the spot. She found herself envious.

"Why do you keep bringing the other lords' trash to my hell?" the Reaper asked.

"I brought Heather for the same reason I brought Malice," Conryu said. "I don't want her soul ending up in some other hell. If she's here, she can't be summoned to cause me more trouble."

"I already sold my soul to her," Heather said. "It's too late to stop her from claiming it."

"Incorrect," his ugly demon book said. "You still have your soul, it has simply been corrupted and linked to Ardent Lilly's hell so when you die, she can claim it."

"Denying the whore a soul is always a good thing," the Reaper said. "Maybe I'll toss this one in the soul jar for a few thousand years."

Conryu shrugged. "As long as she's not causing trouble I don't care where she ends up. I need to get the president out of here before he suffers any permanent damage. Could you send us back to where I was?"

He and the president vanished, leaving Heather alone with the Reaper. Not at all a pleasant situation. An irresistible force dragged her closer to him. She stopped a few feet away from the throne. His power overwhelmed her senses but still she couldn't faint.

"My Chosen is overly kind. You dared to cause trouble on my Earth. For that you shall suffer an eternity of agony."

Pain that made the bomb spell feel like a tickle crashed through her, but only for an instant. Then it vanished and she felt whole again. Heather frowned. Something strange had happened to her and she couldn't put her finger on what.

"Turn around," the Reaper said.

She slowly spun and found a mirror hanging in the air. The Reaper had transformed her beautiful body into the hunched-over, wrinkled body of a crone. Her hair hung lank and patchy gray, her legs bowed and skinny. She was ugly. Uglier than anyone she had ever seen.

No punishment could be worse than this. And that was doubtless exactly what the Reaper intended.

Conryu stepped out of a hell portal a few yards from the gathered rich and powerful. The crowd was staring at what little remained of the mansion. Conryu winced. While technically no one could blame him for what happened, he still felt at least somewhat responsible. At this rate he was going to level every mansion in the neighborhood.

The president, floating beside him on a disk of light magic, remained unconscious. Conryu sent healing energy through him. The visit to Hell hadn't lasted long, but better safe than sorry.

"Conryu!" Kelsie came running over and hugged him. "I was so worried. Is everything okay?"

"For the moment, I think so. Thanks for helping Kai save everyone."

"I didn't do much other than yell that there was a bomb."

"Well, it worked, that's the main thing. I hope Mr. Durst has insurance, though I doubt this sort of thing is covered."

"Hey!" A group of security agents was heading his way. "That girl said you'd keep the president safe. Why is he unconscious?"

"Relax, he just got a bit overwhelmed by the Reaper's presence. It happens. He isn't injured and I'm sure he'll wake up in an hour or two. Rest assured, if we hadn't shifted to Hell, he wouldn't have ever woken up." They were all staring at him, something which happened far too often for his liking. "Are you planning to leave him floating at my side forever or what?"

That snapped them out of their funk and they hastened to collect their charge and hurry away.

Conryu shook his head. "Not even a thank-you. Typical."

"Can you tell me what this was all about?" Kelsie asked.

"Sure. Let's head back to your place. I could use a snack. Maybe Maria would like to join us, she should be done for the day."

"Oh, that sounds fun. You go get her and I'll have the cook fix us something."

"Deal, see you later." They parted ways and he headed for the Kanes' apartment. Looked like he'd survived another mission. There couldn't be that many temples left to purify. At least he hoped not.

EPILOGUE

Conryu appeared in the hall outside the Kanes' apartment. Hopefully Maria hadn't gone to bed yet. Spending an evening with her and Kelsie would make a nice change of pace from fighting and purifying corruption, especially if Kelsie's chef made all his favorites. Rather than knock, he got out his phone and dialed Maria's number.

After three rings she picked up. "Hey, what's up?"

"I'm outside the door at your place. Want to join me for a snack and chat at Kelsie's?"

"I'm still at the office."

He frowned. Eight had come and gone a while ago. "Why?"

"The rune circles you found are fascinating. I've been trying to figure out what they all do and lost track of time. Why don't you come over and pick me up? I could use a break."

"Sure, just a sec." He traveled via the library and emerged in her office moments later. She looked up from her computer monitor as he stepped out of the library. Even from a distance her bloodshot eyes looked bad. "How long have you been staring at that computer?"

"I have no idea. Once I get going, I lose all track of time. How have you been doing?"

Conryu grinned. "That's a bit of a loaded question. I'll tell you over a plate of homemade fries at Kelsie's. Come on."

Maria was about to shut down her computer when an especially shrill beep went off.

"What the hell?" he asked.

"It's an emergency email. I need to check it." Conryu moved closer as she clicked on the icon. "Heaven's mercy."

A badly mangled corpse filled the screen. Someone had tortured the guy in every way conceivable. What sort of person did something like that?

"The message came from the Central PD," Maria said. "The body had a lingering aura of corruption and a mark they couldn't identify. Hang on, there's another picture."

She clicked on it and the breath caught in Conryu's throat when a bloody scythe appeared. Someone had carved it into the dead man's arm, right where the Reaper had marked him.

"I'm not sure what it means," Maria said. "Have you seen anything like it?"

Conryu held out his arm and she gasped. "It's the Reaper's mark. Looks like someone is calling me out."

AUTHOR NOTE

Hello everyone,

It was another rough one for Conryu and the gang, but I enjoyed bring Heather back of a villain cameo and I think she definitely got the punishment she deserved.

If you don't want to miss any of my new releases, deals, general news about the Etherverse, you can signup for my newsletter on my website.
www.jamesewisher.com

Until next time, thanks for reading,

James E. Wisher

The Fate of The Five Kingdoms

The Plague Lands

Elfhome

The 72 Demons

The Blood of Solomon

A Friend in Need

The Demon Masks

Hunt For The Devil Man

The Immortal Apprentice Trilogy

The War With Audin (Prequel Novella)

The Hunt For Revenge

The Army of Darkness

The Apprentice Reborn

The Soul Bound Saga

An Unwelcome Journey

Darkness in Tiber

Depths of Betrayal

The Black Iron Empire

Overmage

The Divine Key Trilogy

Shadow Magic

For The Greater Good

The Divine Key Awakens

The Portal Wars Saga

The Hidden Tower

The Great Northern War

The Portal Thieves

The Master of Magic

The Chamber of Eternity

The Heart of Alchemy

The Sanguine Scroll

Shadow of The Dragons

The Dragonspire Chronicles

The Black Egg

The Mysterious Coin

The Dragons' Graveyard

The Slave War

The Sunken Tower

The Dragon Empress

The Dragonspire Chronicles Omnibus Vol. 1

The Dragonspire Chronicles Omnibus Vol. 2

The Complete Dragonspire Chronicles Omnibus

Soul Force Saga

Disciples of the Horned One Trilogy:

Darkness Rising

Raging Sea and Trembling Earth

Harvest of Souls

Disciples of the Horned One Omnibus

Chains of the Fallen Arc:

Dreaming in the Dark

On Blackened Wings

Chains of the Fallen Omnibus

The Complete Soul Force Saga Omnibus

Other Fantasy Novels:

The Squire

Death and Honor Omnibus

The Rogue Star Series:

Children of Darkness

Children of the Void

Children of Junk

Rogue Star Omnibus Vol. 1

Children of the Black Ship

Children of The End

ABOUT THE AUTHOR

James E. Wisher is a writer of science fiction and Fantasy novels. He's been writing since high school and reading everything he could get his hands on for as long as he can remember.